Julio's Twins

To Brian - who now must take the girls to Italy

MICHAEL MILONE

michael milone

ARENA PRESS
NOVATO, CA

For information about ordering additional quantities, contact:
Arena Press (a division of Academic Therapy Publications)
20 Commercial Blvd., Novato, CA 94949
(800) 422-7249

Library of Congress Control Number: 2012912089

ISBN: 978-1-57128-646-8

10 09 08 07 06 05 04 03 02 01

Printed in the U.S.A.

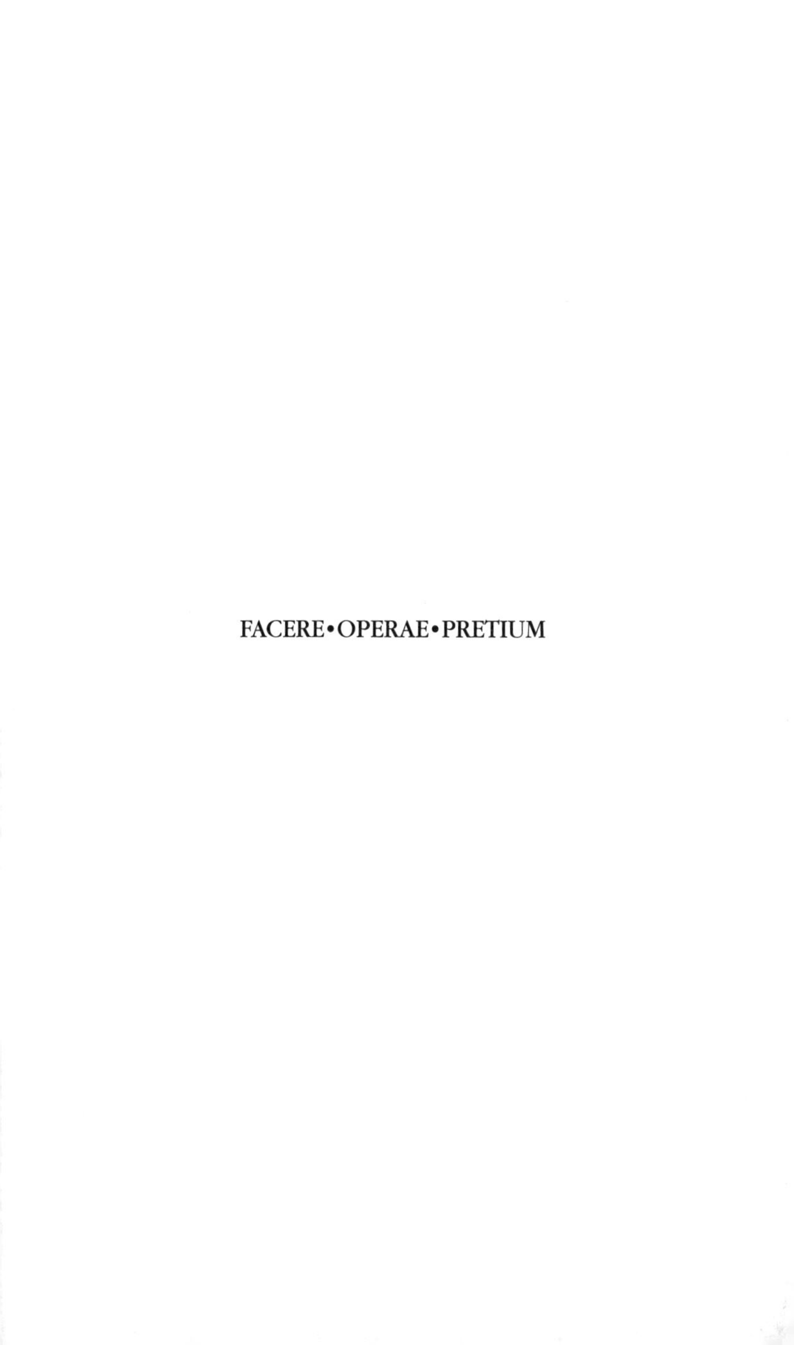

FACERE • OPERAE • PRETIUM

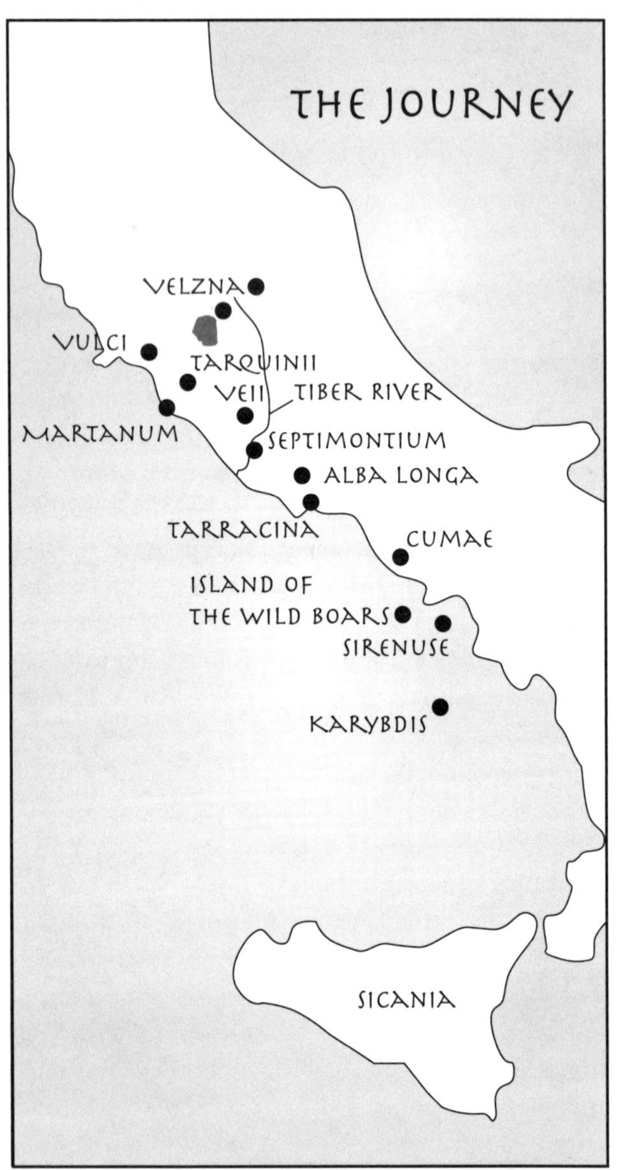
THE JOURNEY
VELZNA
VULCI
TARQUINII
VEII
TIBER RIVER
MARTANUM
SEPTIMONTIUM
ALBA LONGA
TARRACINA
CUMAE
ISLAND OF
THE WILD BOARS
SIRENUSE
KARYBDIS
SICANIA

Prologue

Having learned the art of writing, I am able to tell this story so that others may know of our history. It is about two brothers, Romulus and Remus. Because of them, our people have survived and have made a village on a hill beside the Tiber River. I was there when all of these events took place, and there is no reason to doubt the truth of this tale. I am Serena, the sister of Romulus and Remus.

In our time, the gods and other fantastic creatures walked among humans. I do not know if this will be true in your time, so you may find what I say difficult to believe.

Although the gods are immortal, they cannot take pleasure in countless things in life that we enjoy every day, especially our feelings. In order to experience our sensations, they sometimes take the form of humans, or even animals. As strange as this sounds, it seems to satisfy them.

The gods are not alone in meddling in human affairs. Demons and phantoms plague us also, enjoying the agony to which they subject us. They often steal the souls of humans and take them to the Underworld, where they remain forever.

The gods sometimes helped humans, as in the case of Ceres, who taught us how to plant and sow. In many cases, however, the immortals were more mischievous, waging their personal battles with one another through us. There is no better example than the war between the Greeks and the Trojans. Our troubles were caused by some of the gods, but our triumph was accomplished in part by the intervention of others, primarily Juno, who holds a special place among our people and will never be forgotten.

That is not to say that the gods controlled every aspect of our existence. For much of the time, we lived everyday lives. Our people had their huts near Alba Longa for many generations, where they enjoyed the bounty of the land. We raised cattle and sheep in addition to harvesting wheat, beans, and other plants. We lived in peace with our neighbors and traded with the Greeks, who sometimes visited us. All of that changed when Discordia, the goddess of strife, disrupted our lives.

Chapter I

For hundreds of years, Discordia had been the most unhappy goddess on Olympus. She had been vexed since the end of the Trojan War, a conflict she had helped to begin.

"Humans have disappointed me," she said to the Keres who surrounded her. "We must help them become more hostile to one another."

The Keres were death spirits who thrived on conflict. They sought the souls of those who died while inflicting harm on others, and nothing pleased them more than when Discordia drove humans to violence.

Juno, the queen of the gods, knew of Discordia's plan to torment a small group of humans who lived in a simple village. She also knew she could not directly interfere with another god's whims. Juno chose another way to side with the humans who had for so long honored her.

I remember well the day on which my brothers were born, although I was just a few years old at the time. The morning was clear and beautiful, but by the afternoon, storm clouds had filled the sky. Thunder and lightning signaled their birth that night, almost as if the gods were welcoming them.

When my mother's time to give birth was near, the midwife came to help her. She was accompanied by a kind stranger who brought with him a young dog. He said the *canis*, which was of the herding breed often employed by shepherds in our region, was a gift for the boys. He departed, and I was puzzled at his words, for the boys had not yet been born.

Romulus was born first. The midwife presented him to my father, Faustulus. He brought the baby outside and held him up to the sky as an offering to the gods. This is the tradition of our people. The shouts of the midwife brought him back into the hut where my *pater* witnessed the birth of his second son. My *mater*, Laurentia, urged my father to return outside to show the gods both boys. He did not, however, and stayed by my mother's side, anxious about her well-being after giving birth twice. I have sometimes wondered if his concern for my mother angered some of the gods and brought their wrath upon us.

From the beginning, the twins—the *gemelli*—were different from other children. They were inseparable, and from the moment of their birth, they were followed everywhere by Nivea, the dog brought by the stranger. Their early years were unremarkable, as were mine, and our lives were little different from those of our friends.

Nivea received her name because of her color, which was white as snow. She grew quickly from a playful puppy to a strong and dependable guardian of the *gemelli* and the significant people in their lives. It would not be for many years that we would understand the truth about her.

For a time, our village had no name, as we were not many families, but we were often called Albans. Like other villages nearby, we depended for many things on Alba Longa, a much larger town not far away. The people of Alba Longa spoke Latin, our language, so we could understand them easily. Our families could trade the products of our fields and animals for certain foods or goods we could not make ourselves.

It was also in Alba Longa that we came to know the Greeks, people from far across the sea. They were good people, at least to us, and they taught us much. From them we learned many of the stories about the gods. The Greek language was different from ours, but some of us learned it, and they knew the language that we spoke.

Not far from our home was another group of people, the Etruscans. Like the Greeks, they spoke a language different from ours, but unlike the Greeks, they were sometimes unfriendly to us. We were unimportant to them, and because of their numbers and strength of arms, they believed they ruled us. This belief was not much of a burden to us, because we rarely saw any of their warriors or even their merchants. More will be said of the Etruscans, but if I speak ill of them, I realize now that what they did to us was not wholly their fault.

The Albans were loosely allied with the Etruscans. A major road from the Etruscan lands in the north to their southern outposts passed close to Alba Longa. If the Albans wanted to, they might have prevented movement on the road, which would have made things difficult for the Etruscans. The trade that the road brought to Alba Longa, however, made such a move foolish. The Etruscans were responsible for the success of the Albans.

Our homes were plain structures made of wood and mud with a thatched roof of straw. They were perfectly suited to the weather in our region, where cold and snow were rare. The houses required no special materials or talents to build. If the weather or a stray animal damaged one, it was easily repaired.

We ate what we could grow or obtain through trade. Our herds of cattle, sheep, and goats grazed on the hills and valleys that surrounded our village. We kept the animals away from our wheat fields, which gave us seeds that we ground for flour. Each home had a small garden plot. In a good year, we could raise some vegetables in almost every season. Fruit trees grew wild nearby, and in their season, provided us with apples, pears, apricots, figs, and cherries.

The Greeks brought us a new tree, the olive. Some of these trees grew wild in our area, but the Greeks showed us how to cultivate them in orchards. Our trees are still young, but they are already producing olives. They promised to show us how to cause the olives to lose their bitter taste and how to crush them for their oil. My father believed that this oil would be valuable for trading with the Greeks and others.

We were not as wealthy as other people to the north were. Though our hills were good for growing things and raising animals, the hills of the Etruscans had iron, a metal that could be turned into tools and weapons. The Greeks and Phoenicians prized this metal. They were even willing to trade gold for it. Iron makes tools that are stronger than those of stone, copper, or bronze. The people of our village mostly used tools made of stone. They were not as strong as metal tools, but they were easily made. Only a few of the men of our village had metal weapons.

Like the other young people in our settlement, Romulus and Remus were expected at an early age to work in the fields with the rest of the family. They had a special knack for tending sheep and cattle. Maybe this was because of the talents of Nivea. Dogs like her were developed to help shepherds, and she had a way with animals that defied explanation.

By the time the boys grew into their teenage years, stories about them had spread to other villages. The tale of the twins, the dog, and the storm that coincided with their birth became exaggerated, as on a day when we visited Alba Longa to trade. This day has special meaning for all of us, because it was the beginning of a sequence of events that, to this day, I find hard to believe. I suspect that all of you who read this story will agree with me.

"We were not raised by a wolf," sighed Romulus. He shook his head and looked at his brother, who rolled his eyes. The twins had been hearing this story for as long as they could remember.

My brothers and I were standing in an open space in the center of the town. We had brought wool to trade for cloth and knives made of iron. We would spend the night in the town with relatives and then return to our settlement where our parents, Faustulus and Laurentia, were awaiting us.

Surrounding us was a group of young people about our age. All of them had heard of the twins—the *gemelli*—and the unusual circumstances of their birth. It was said that a wolf had waited near the family's shelter, and within days of their birth, had stolen both of them to be raised as her pups. As absurd as this sounds, it was a common belief.

"Nivea is a dog, not a *lupus*," added Remus. "She was there the night we were born, waiting outside the hut as she does every night. She is standing beside us now. From a distance, she looks a little like a wolf because of her size. We are no different from any of you who has a family dog."

"That is not the story I know," said a tall girl leaning on a spear at the edge of the crowd. "We heard that you were part wolf, and that when the moon was full, you ran with a pack of wolves."

The rest of the group stepped back from the twins. Those who had weapons put their hands on them, but they did not draw them. The tall girl, however, did not back away.

"Our cousin Chiara has an impressive imagination," said Romulus. "I wish she would use it to create stories about the Greeks or the Etruscans and not about her family." Romulus lunged toward Chiara, laughing as he did. But she was too quick. She had anticipated his move and stepped aside, tripping him with her spear. Laughing, she dodged behind her friends, who now saw that the stories she had been telling them were completely untrue.

Chiara is my age, and in many ways, was a second sister to the *gemelli*. She often stayed with us, and we stayed with her family when we were in Alba Longa. We would spend this night with them before heading home in the morning. She is both strong and beautiful. Many families in Alba Longa have tried to arrange a marriage with her for their sons. She has resisted all of these offers. She told me in confidence that she wants to experience some excitement before settling down. For her to do so would be unconventional, because among our people, a woman is expected to become a wife and have children.

After this encounter in the square, we completed our trades. Chiara stayed with us, because she enjoyed our company. For our part, we liked having her around. She knew many of the traders and helped us make fair exchanges. From the way the men treated her, it was easy to see that she was one of their favorites.

"So, my cousins, what is our next adventure?" asked Chiara, as she ran a hand over Nivea's back. "Nivea and I need some drama in our lives."

"Why do you think we want an adventure?" asked Remus. "Is it not enough that that we protect our flocks, trade when we can, and put up with you making up stories about us?"

"You have settled into an acceptable life," answered Chiara. "Don't you long for uncertainty? Think of the Greeks who trade with us. They risk everything to travel across the sea from their home, which is who knows where. They have seen all the lands where the legends have happened. If we get out of sight of Alba Longa, we feel as if we have had an adventure, yet it is just a day's walk away."

"We are shepherds," answered Romulus. "With the help of Nivea, we tend our flocks. When the crops mature, we harvest them and earn a share of what we gather. We have no big plans for our lives. What do you want us to do, join the Etruscans to battle the Umbrians? Perhaps we could sail with the Greeks to seek a newer world. You are different, Chiara. Your heart is elsewhere, and your dreams are exciting. I wish that we had your spirit, but we don't. We are more boring than you are, and you are going to have to put up with us."

As I look back on my brother's words, I realize that they were ironic and in a sense prescient. Within a day, our lives changed forever, and dare I say, so did the *historia* of our people.

Chapter II

With the Keres at her side, Discordia brought herself to Earth not far from Alba Longa. She looked for some humans who would be convinced by her words. She chose the people of Veii, a cluster of villages on the north side of the Tiber River.

The Veiians were one of the Etruscan tribes, people who lived in the central part of the land that would be known as Italia. Unlike the other Etruscans, they had no metals to trade. They were very successful farmers and produced food that was prized by many other tribes. They also had a second important resource: salt. They obtained salt from deposits beside the great sea. Through the actions of Discordia, the Veiians became hostile toward their neighbors.

We spent the night with Chiara and her family. While we sat around the cooking fire, we spoke of the people of Veii. In the last year, they had become more combative. They had always been much stronger than the people who lived near them. For whatever reason, they seemed to be more aggressive lately. The Veiians had absorbed the tribe called the Falisci, who were now their subjects. We worried that they might do the same with those of us who live in the small villages. We really didn't want this to happen because we liked things the way they were. What could they possibly gain by taking over our lands during these difficult times?

In the morning, we went back to our settlement. Chiara joined us. She had no real responsibilities at home on this day. She also knew that we could use her help with sheep shearing and picking our crops.

The wool from the few sheep we had left was very important. With it, we could trade for food. Times were hard, however, and there were few sheep. A drought had started the year before, and both plants and animals had been affected. There was barely enough food for us to get by. The only reason we had any sheep at all was because of a small spring near our home. Coincidentally, the spring began to flow on the day that Nivea arrived. From that day onward, our village was called Fontis because of the spring. We were all very proud that we had a name.

"Have you noticed that Nivea does not seem to get older as the years pass?" Chiara asked. As she spoke, Nivea turned her head as if she understood.

"She is a remarkable dog," answered Remus, "and we have often wondered about the same thing. She is as frisky as ever. Serena remembers her earliest days with us."

"Everything about her is odd," I said. "The stranger who brought her simply dropped by as if he were delivering her especially to us. Nivea was a puppy, but she took to us as if she had known us her whole life. I can't remember a day that she has ever been away from the *gemelli*, and as you mentioned, she has not aged at all since she matured."

The walk back home was uneventful at first. We saw almost no one, which was a surprise. The road we were on connected several outlying villages with Alba Longa. Under normal circumstances, the road would be busy with people walking, riding horses, or carrying goods in carts to and from the center where trading took place. Even the Greek traders sometimes used the tree-lined *via*, but not on this day. We thought nothing of it.

The road climbed the crest of a hill from where we could see our village. We could find no words to describe the sight that greeted us. Smoke and flames rose from the village, and men on horseback were sweeping through the huts swinging their swords. We could see from their weapons and horses that they were Veiians. There were only about ten of them, but the people of our village were no match for them.

Without thinking, we ran toward the village. We had no serious weapons, other than the long staffs we carried and Chiara's spear. None of us were trained as warriors, but that did not matter. Our people needed help, and we had to do what we could.

What happened next was unsettling to the Veiians. The four of us running down the hill, plus a large dog, must have seemed to them to be an armed force of warriors. Several of them broke off their attack on the village and came toward us, but they did not seem confident.

"Serena and Chiara, run off toward the trees on the left with Nivea!" shouted Romulus. "The fig trees in the grove are close together. They will not be able to get to you on horseback. Let the lead rider come to us."

Romulus and Remus had no weapons other than the sticks they carried, but they knew how to use them. Thieves on foot or on horseback occasionally tried to steal sheep and cattle, so they had some experience fighting. Even so, they seemed overmatched against armed riders on horses.

The two of them stood side by side until the first horseman drew near. They separated quickly. The rider, who had his sword in his right hand, tried first to slash at Romulus. As the horseman leaned to his right to do this, Remus swung his staff and knocked him off the horse. Stunned at the attack, the rider tumbled off clumsily, injuring himself in the fall. He couldn't get to his feet quickly. Romulus picked up his sword from the ground and slashed him. The rider lay on the ground bleeding.

"I'll grab the horse," said Remus. He walked to the horse, which without a rider, had slowed down. He calmed the horse before jumping onto its back.

"Here, take the sword," said Romulus. He held the bloody blade of the sword and pointed the hilt at his brother. Grasping the sword in his left hand, Remus waited for the next horseman.

In the meantime, Chiara, Nivea, and I had reached the inside of the grove of fig trees. A Veiian saw us and hurried toward us on horseback. Seeing that he could not ride among the trees, he dismounted and ran toward us, furious that his companion had been killed. He could not have made a more deadly mistake.

"Be patient, Nivea," I said to the growling dog. "Let him come to us."

The warrior slashed his sword at the branches that were in his way and strode aggressively toward us. Even though Chiara held a spear, it must have seemed primitive to him, being made of rough wood and having a stone point.

When he reached the trees just in front of us, several thick branches blocked his way. They kept him from moving his sword efficiently. It was then that I said to Nivea, "Get him."

The white *canis* ran full speed toward the man, who could not see her clearly or slash at her with his sword because of the branches. She knocked him off his feet, grabbed his throat in her jaws, and crushed it. She swung her head back and forth, snapping his neck.

"Come, Serena, catch his horse," said my cousin. She made her way through the trees, and as she did, she picked up the man's sword and tucked it into her belt.

Nivea and I followed her, both of us glancing back to be sure the Veiian was dead. He did not move, his head rested at a horrible angle to his body, and blood seeped from his throat. A gruesome form, one of the Keres I am sure, hovered near him, undoubtedly stealing his soul. No end could have been more fitting for such a terrible man.

We reached the edge of the grove just as Romulus came from the other direction. Like Remus, he mounted the horse, but had no weapon. Seeing this, Chiara said, "Take my spear," and she tossed it lightly to him.

"But you have no weapon," he argued, and he tried to hand it back to her.

"I have the Veiian's sword," she answered. "Because of Nivea, he won't have any further use for it."

Pulling on the reins, Romulus wheeled the horse around and headed toward his *frater*,

Remus. Nivea ran beside him. Together, the three of them turned to face the remaining Veiians, who had been held up by resistance from the villagers.

But the Veiians did not advance toward my brothers and Nivea. The attackers looked at one another with perplexed expressions that quickly turned to unease. Two of their comrades had been slain somehow, and these boys had their horses and weapons. The boys were the *gemelli* they had heard so much about, along with a dog whose jaws dripped with blood. The Veiians were familiar with *augurium*, the study of omens. They thought these signs meant that the gods were with the boys. They circled their horses, urged them on, and retreated, not even looking back at the village that they had ravaged.

Chiara and I ran to the *gemelli*, who helped us climb onto the horses. None of us said a word, still shocked as we were by what had happened. With Nivea at our side, we rode to what was left of our settlement. The wounded were everywhere, and two more Veiians lay dead on the ground. Most of the huts had been damaged, and a few small fires burned. Those who were uninjured fought the fires and began to tend to the wounded. We dismounted and helped in any way we could.

"Your father and I were so worried about you," said Laurentia, our mother. She was caring for one of the older people who had been wounded. "The Veiians came out of nowhere and attacked us. We didn't know if the same thing was happening in other villages."

"It might have been," said Chiara. "As we walked along the road, we didn't see a single person, but we thought nothing of it."

Using wet branches and buckets of water brought from the spring, the people of my village soon extinguished the fires set by the attackers. The two dead Veiians were dragged from the village, but not before being stripped of their weapons. On a barren piece of ground, a pile of brush and wood was built. The bodies of the Veiians were placed on top of the pile, and more brush and wood was added. The brush was ignited, and their bodies were consumed in the flames.

The burning of the bodies was not an act of vengeance. Cremation was a common way to treat the dead. The promptness with which the bodies were cremated was not exceptional, either. In order to prevent disease, cremation was usually done as quickly as possible.

Back in the village, we tried to help the wounded. Fortunately, their injuries were not serious. The Veiian warriors were so driven by a mysterious force that they were careless in their use of weapons. Their mindless anger caused them to be in such a frenzy that their blows and slashes were awkward. Certainly, they wrecked many huts, but that was more a result of their poor riding than their intent. It was almost as if they were possessed and were acting under the control of an evil spirit.

A peculiar thing happened as we tended those who were injured. Nivea went from person to person, snuggling her head against them and almost forcing them to stroke her back. This brought a sense of peace to the wounded, and their pain seemed to become less. The frightened children were calmer, and their parents were better able to soothe them.

The four of us stood together, and Nivea wandered back to us. It was only now that the events of the day began to sink in. We looked at each other not knowing what to say. It was then that Massimo, the leader of our village, came to us.

"You have saved our people. Were it not for you, the Veiians might have killed all of us."

Several of our friends about our own age stood behind him. They nodded their heads in agreement and began a stream of questions.

"Where did you learn to fight?"

"Can you show us how to dismount a rider?"

"How did Nivea get blood on her face?"

Even Chiara and I were taken aback by my brothers' actions. It was just the night before that the *gemelli* had insisted that they were just shepherds, and that they had no need for adventure. Yet today, when faced with an overwhelming challenge, they had behaved in a way that could not be explained. They seemed to have been guided by a spirit of greatness that was completely unexpected. For the first time, I began to believe that there was something about my brothers that none of us understood.

Chapter III

Discordia watched the mayhem she had caused in the village from a hill in the distance. Although she took some pleasure in the event, her annoyance was clear.

"The Veiians were more cowardly than I had hoped. They should never have allowed themselves to be driven off by a bunch of shepherds. But my Keres had some souls to feast on, so they are happy for now."

Turning to her minions, she murmured, "There will soon be more souls. Do not be discouraged."

For the rest of the day, we fixed the huts as best we could and cared for the injured. Guards armed with the weapons of the Veiian attackers were posted around the village. We weren't sure what we would do if they returned, especially with reinforcements, but thinking that we were guarded made us feel better.

At nightfall, we gathered together for a small meal. The raiders had ruined the food storage area, which had not held much to begin with. It was only then that we realized how difficult our lives had become. We did not have enough food to survive the coming winter. Many of our people were injured, and at least half the huts in our village would have to be replaced.

"We can get through this," insisted Remus. "The huts can be rebuilt, and we have some things we can trade for food. Some of us can work for other villages during the harvest in exchange for food. The drought has not harmed them as much as us."

My brother's words were encouraging, and with them in mind, we dozed off into fitful sleep. It is not an exaggeration to say that throughout the night, all of us who were unhurt awoke periodically and wandered around protectively. We could not rid ourselves of the image of the Veiian raid. Ours had long been a peaceful village, and the viciousness of their attack was unsettling.

The morning was no different from the day before. We repaired the least damaged huts first so that several families could share them. None of the injured had serious wounds, so fewer of us had to tend to them. Most of us searched for food. We were fortunate because the fig trees still held much fruit, and our hunters returned with a huge boar.

Massimo and Faustulus, along with several of the other men, were absent for most of the morning. We thought they were patrolling around the village looking for Veiians. At the midday meal, they returned. Massimo was silent, which bothered me. He and my father were usually talkative during the meal. They liked to get my friends and me to talk about whatever interested us. They also would ask the elders to speak of the past so we could learn the stories of our tribe. At the end of the meal, Massimo rose and addressed us.

"We were lucky yesterday that none of us died at the hands of the Veiians. Even so, our future is in doubt. Some of the elders and I have discussed the matter, and we have a difficult decision to make."

Those of us listening to Massimo recognized that he was about to make a serious announcement. We had no idea, however, how his words would impact us. Chiara and I looked at my brothers and shrugged our shoulders. I glanced around at the others, who like us, were anxious about what he would say.

"Our village has little hope of survival the way things are now," continued Massimo. "The drought has affected our crops and our animals. There is just one choice that the elders and I think will work. We must follow the old ways and sunder the village according to the legend of the Lydians."

Although we all knew the story of the Lydians, we were unclear about exactly what Massimo meant. As the story goes, hundreds of years before, the people of Lydia near Greece suffered a famine. Under King Atys, they split the people into two groups. They drew lots, with one group staying and one group leaving. The group that left their home built ships and sailed to a new land. Some people believe they were our ancestors.

"What are you saying?" asked Romulus. "We can't split the village."

"We can, and we must," answered Massimo. "Here is what we have decided. Those between the ages of twelve and nineteen who are unmarried will leave the village. The adults, the very young, and the eldest will stay. The adults can care for the young and the old, while the teenagers can find other places where they can work and live. This is the hardest decision I have ever made."

Don't think badly of Massimo and the others for what they did. Their decision truly was our only option. And among our people, teenagers are supposed to behave in many ways as adults. Some of us marry and have children, and all of us work with the adults. We know how to use tools and weapons, and we are not at all like some of the other people who expect little of the *adolescentis* in their teenage years.

Massimo's words were a stunning blow to all of us. The village was our home, and these were our people. The sense of loss I felt was indescribable. Instinctively, I put my arm around Chiara, who sat beside me. Even though she was not of our village, tears rolled down her face. She was not alone; the parents of my friends wept openly. After a moment, however, Romulus stood up and spoke words that were unforgettable.

"As painful as this decision is for all of us, it is probably the only real choice we have. We must make the best of it. Those of us who have to leave are often away from the village for many days. True, we get to come home after a time, but every single one of us has experienced life outside the village."

He paused and looked around before speaking again. "The children and elders must be cared for, which is the responsibility of the adults. We who must leave will also take care of one another."

Then Remus stood up and added his thoughts. "We will not be gone forever. Unlike the Lydians, we will not sail away never to return. We may not have to go far to find a place to settle, and we can stay in touch with our families. The rain will fall again some day as it did in the past, and we may choose to return. We will never forget our home and our people."

Hearing his words, those of us who had to leave stood up. More than twenty of us crowded around Romulus and Remus, standing as tall as we could. The youngest of us would have the most difficult time, for they were most dependent on their parents. Nonetheless, they stood with us, holding back their tears.

Chiara joined us, but in contrast to the others, she seemed contented. "This is my dream," she insisted, "an adventure with my friends and cousins. It is time for me to leave my parents' home anyway, and I cannot think of anything that offers more promise than to travel with you. I hope that you will let me join you."

The words of Romulus, Remus, and Chiara changed everything. A few minutes before, all of us were upset. Now, as painful as leaving our home would be, things did not seem so disastrous. The youngest of the group were less skilled in some ways than the rest of us, but we would protect them. We were not going away never to return, and for all we knew, we would end up in another village not far away. All of us had visited other settlements for days at a time, and we had friends or family in many of them. We had traded with Greeks, Umbrians, Falisci, and even the Etruscans. We were going to make the best of this situation.

Timidly, I turned to Massimo and asked, "When should we prepare to leave?"

"In a few days," he responded kindly. "That will give us time to say goodbye and find provisions for your journey. There is no hurry."

"Without being disrespectful, I disagree with Massimo," said Remus. "Because of the drought and the attack, there are no provisions for us. What food is available should be kept here for the youngest and the eldest. We can forage on our way to wherever we go."

Romulus agreed with his brother. "Staying here for even one more *dies* is going to make our leaving more unpleasant. We can each take a little food, a cloak, and a weapon. Anything more will be an additional burden. If it is to be done at all, then let it be done quickly."

"But where will you go?" asked my mother, Laurentia.

"There is only one direction that is feasible," replied Remus. "We must go south. The Veiians and their allies almost surround us in the other directions. I don't know if they will harass us, but I would rather not take the chance. There are fewer mountains to the south, I have heard, and there are more Greek towns. They have always treated us well, and most of us speak a little Greek, at least."

"You have spoken wisely," said Massimo, "and bravely. We are all grateful that you have made this separation less difficult. Heading south is the most practical course. There will be less danger, more opportunities to forage for food, and a better chance of encountering friendly Greeks. They have a settlement in Cumae, and you will have no trouble finding it. I have been there myself, and I can make you a map."

My father then suggested, "Won't you at least

take the horses of the Veiians? They can carry supplies to make the journey easier. Some of the youngest of you can ride them."

A small voice interrupted their conversation. "If Romulus and Remus are going to walk, then I could never ride." It was Nico, the youngest of the teens.

"Nor could I," said Anna, a slight girl whose affection for Nico was the cause of much teasing for both of them. There was no mistaking the determination of her words, however.

"You need the horses more than we do," contended Remus. "If we took them, we would have to worry about food and water for them. We must travel with as few *impedimenta* as possible."

Chiara, who was the most eager of any of us, then said, "Let's grab what we can and get started. There is much of the day left. My village is toward the south, and we can be there by nightfall. I can say goodbye to my family and friends, and we'll have at least one night of safety. Oh, and my mother and the other women of the village will want to make us a huge dinner. We'll have leftovers for days."

The decision made, the family groups headed to their shelters, or what was left of them. We picked up the few things that each of us would carry on our journey to wherever we might settle. My parents found a little food for us, and each of us took one outer garment. Chiara, because she had come from her village, had her spear and cloak. She insisted that she needed no food other than what she already carried.

Each of us had a small water pouch made of animal skin. There were plenty of water sources to the south, but we were not sure if we could get to them because of the Veiians. We still did not know if their anger had been directed only at us or at other villages, too. This uncertainty also meant that we could not travel by the main road. We'd have to follow the smaller trails that were rarely used. This would slow us down, but it was much safer.

It was not long before we all got together by the spring at the edge of the village. We filled our water skins, made sure we had what we needed, and said our goodbyes. Nivea went from person to person as if she knew what was happening. As had happened the night before, touching her brought a good feeling to those who would stay behind, especially the children.

We set off, with Romulus and Remus at the head of the group. This was somewhat surprising, because they were not the eldest or the strongest of the boys. The events of the previous day, however, gave them a special place among us. There was no discussion about leadership; the role simply fell to them.

At first we were silent, but that did not last very long. Small conversations broke out among us, focusing at first on where we would go and what we would do. Those who had not yet visited Chiara's village asked her about it as if they were going on a typical outing. Questions arose about the Greek presence in Cumae, but no one had ever been there. Those of us who had heard stories of the town shared what we knew. Chiara promised that her parents, who had sailed along the coast to Cumae with Greek traders, would tell us more.

"What are you thinking, Serena?" asked Chiara. She had noticed that I had been quiet since leaving the village and had joined in none of the conversations.

"I'm not really thinking. I'm still overcome with the events of the past two days. The attack by the Veiians, the bravery of my brothers, the ferociousness of Nivea, and your fearlessness when the warrior came after us."

"Don't forget, you stood your ground as well as I did," Chiara replied.

"Yes, I did, and I still can't believe it. What has come over all of us? Two days ago, we were giggling at one another. Today, we're setting off to find a new life. It's crazy."

Chapter IV

"They are a determined lot," said Jupiter from Olympus, watching the young people leave their village. He addressed no one in particular, although he was surrounded by many of the other immortals.

The goddess Ceres smiled and added, "They certainly are, and they are so young. It saddens me that Discordia has chosen to test them so harshly."

"Yet they have not once questioned their destiny," continued Jupiter. "It speaks well of them."

When we reached the outskirts of her village late in the afternoon, Chiara ran ahead to a group of people collecting honey from hives kept near some fruit trees. Her village, Apia, was named for the bees that the villagers raised. From a distance, she could see that one of the people was her mother. Chiara realized that such a large group of strangers approaching the village was unusual, and she did not want anyone to be concerned.

"What is this?" asked Julia, after hugging her daughter. "Have you brought the entire village of Fontis?"

"Only the teenagers, including my cousins. I will explain later. Mother, have any Veiian warriors attacked our village?" By then, the rest of us had reached Chiara, and we overheard her question.

"What are you asking, Chiara? The Veiians have no interest in us, and they did not attack us. No armed force has been here."

"Mother, have you heard news of any of the other villages being attacked?"

"None that I know of. Several traders have come through our village today, and none of them mentioned attacks by the Veiians. Why are you asking?"

Julia's answer puzzled us. It seemed as if the Veiians had singled us out for an attack, yet they had no reason to do so. Our people were harmless to them, and we had nothing of any value, other than our tools and food supplies, both of which were nothing compared to what the Veiians had. The attack on our village made no sense.

Because Chiara's village was not far from ours, many of us had visited there. And like us, some of our friends had family in this settlement. When we went to the village itself, we were greeted warmly, but no one had any idea why we had come. Chiara brought us to the large open space among the huts and asked the villagers to gather around, which they did. As Chiara had guessed, her mother and some of the women suggested that we eat something. We thought that was a great idea. Our day had been long, and the idea of spending time with them sounded perfect.

The food and the presence of visitors brought just about everyone to the center of the village. Chiara attempted to tell the story of the Veiian attack on Fontis, but she was interrupted often by our companions. They insisted on giving the details of how the four of us and Nivea had driven them off. Their praise, I must admit, was flattering, even if they exaggerated a little.

"Our friends make the story seem a lot more impressive than it really was," Chiara insisted. "The Veiians, for whatever reason, broke off the attack." But by then the people of her village had been convinced of our bravery, and they looked at us in a different light.

Chiara ended the story by telling of the sundering and how we had been sent off. The mood of the people of Apia changed from curiosity to sympathy by the time she had finished. Like us, they knew the story of the Lydians, and they could not imagine that something like this could happen in our time.

Turning to Varro, the leader of the village, Julia asked, "Why can't they stay here? We have not been attacked, and the drought has been less severe here. Many of them have family among our villagers."

"As much as I would like to say that they can stay, it would be impossible for us to accept all of them," answered Varro. "Were there just five or six, we could make it work, but there are more of you than we can sustain. As things stand, we have barely enough food in storage to get through the winter."

The tone of his voice showed the disappointment that Varro felt. "If things were different, I would offer all of you sanctuary, but that is not an option. Are there any of you who would like to stay?"

His question took us off guard. When we left Fontis, we all assumed that we would be together wherever we went. Now, just a few hours' walk from our home, some of us were given the option of staying. This seemed to be an appealing choice.

No one, however, volunteered to stay. Recognizing that asking for sanctuary might be seen as a sign of cowardice, Remus suggested that we draw straws, a common practice in our time. The five with the longest straws could choose to stay in Apia. If any of them decided not to, the person who selected the next longest straw would have the choice. His suggestion seemed fair and reasonable.

Chiara went to the pile of straw beside her family's hut. She picked up a handful and made sure that one set of ends was more or less even. From this bunch, each of us would draw one straw. She held the bundle with two hands to ensure fairness and walked from one to the other. Each of us drew a single straw.

"Aren't you going to pick one?" asked Nico.

"No, I am not from your village," she answered. "And, I am going with the group no matter what." She turned to her parents and said, "You guessed as much, didn't you?"

Rather than being dismayed, her parents laughed. "We would have been surprised had you said something else," insisted Claudius, her father. "You have been longing for adventure since you could walk. You learned the story of Odysseus after Troy by the time you were five, and every time you heard it, a faraway look came to your eyes. This is your moment. We love you and will miss you, but we understand that you must go."

By now, all of us had drawn our straws. We came together to compare them in front of Varro, who would be an impartial judge. What took place then could not be explained, yet clearly was an omen. All of us had drawn straws of the same length.

At first, we thought it was simply odd. But when we put the straws alongside one another, their similarity became evident. Not a hair's difference could be found among any of them.

"Well," insisted Varro, "you must do it again to see who will stay."

Looking at one another, we all shook our heads and gratefully declined his offer. Like almost everyone in our region, we believed in omens, and our drawing straws of the same length was a clear sign that none of us were meant to stay in Apia. We would remain together and move on as a group.

Night had fallen, and the fire was beginning to die down. Our exhaustion had finally caught up with us, which Julia noticed. "Let's put an end to the evening and let the young people get to sleep. They will have a long day ahead of them tomorrow."

Although we could have stayed in huts with different families, we chose to spend the night together around the fire. The night would be cool, but with the fire and the cloaks we had brought, we would be comfortable. Not long after the people of Apia said goodnight, we were asleep.

"Serena, wake up," whispered Romulus as he shook my shoulder. "Be as quiet and still as you can."

Romulus and Remus were waking all of us, and as they did, they cautioned us to be quiet. Struggling out of a deep sleep, it took several minutes for me to become fully conscious. The night was dark because there was no moon, and the fire had died down to embers. Between the darkness and my half-awake state, I was not sure what I was seeing. Not far from the village, Nivea seemed to be confronting a horrible creature.

"What is that?" I asked. "It looks almost human, but its shape keeps shifting from a beautiful woman to a horrid monster."

"It is Lamia," claimed Chiara. "She has visited our village before."

Hearing the name of the shapeshifting demon sent chills through all of us. Lamia was a horrid beast who ate children. Parents told terrible stories of Lamia when children misbehaved, insisting that this evil spirit would punish them. Most of us lost our outward fear of Lamia as we got older. Because her story is so much a part of our history, she always haunted us inwardly, even though we did not believe she was real.

"Why would Nivea be able to keep her from coming after us?" asked Remus. "She is just a dog, and Lamia is an immortal."

As we watched the confrontation, we realized that Lamia was clutching something in her powerful hands. It was a human form, and even though she was far away, we were able to see who it was. Lamia held our youngest companion, Nico.

Step by step, Nivea kept driving Lamia backward. The demon would lunge forward as if to pass her, but Nivea was too quick. Strangely, they did not attack one another directly. As they moved farther away, an unexpected thing happened. Perhaps it was the dark night, but Nivea seemed to be growing in size and becoming brighter. As she did, Lamia was less able to resist her, until the demon dropped Nico, turned, and fled, disappearing into the shadows.

Nivea ran to the boy who lay on the ground. At first, he did not move, and it saddened me to think that Lamia had taken his life. Nivea licked him, Nico started to move, and then he struggled to his feet. Once he rose, Nivea paced back and forth between him and the escaping Lamia. When she was convinced that the phantom was gone for good, she turned and sidled up to Nico. She nuzzled him, and with the dog at his side, he returned to us. The two of them looked back occasionally, but otherwise seemed not to be afraid. They headed toward us, appearing no different than they had before we had fallen asleep.

At first, we did not know what to do. Chiara, however, responded in a most natural way. She ran to Nico, picked him up, and hugged him. This attention both pleased and embarrassed the boy. She dropped to her knees and hugged Nivea, who whined in the loving way she always did. Chiara's grasp of the situation and her actions were incredible. Not minutes after a near encounter with an immortal, she had reacted with the most basic human emotion, love, and everything was fine.

For his part, Nico was enjoying a moment of celebrity. He remembered little of what happened, other than finding himself in the arms of Lamia. He insisted that he felt no fear because of the intervention of Nivea. Time, he insisted, seemed to stop, and Lamia became powerless. She released him, and an aura of protection coming from Nivea surrounded him. He was reluctant to say so, but he felt protected by the gods.

"You cannot understand what it was like," he declared. "Lamia dropped me as if she had come up against an irresistible force. Nivea was not a dog, but an immortal whose power was much greater than Lamia's. I'm certain that all of this was an imagining, but it seemed so real."

"Our dog never ceases to mystify me," sighed Romulus. "How could she confront an immortal?"

His observation was exactly what I had been thinking, and I am sure others felt the same way. Nivea was now walking from person to person, looking at us carefully before moving on. Satisfied we were all safe, she settled herself where she had been before, at the edge of the group, with her back to the fire, looking for anyone who might approach us. To someone unfamiliar with the events that just took place, it would seem that nothing had happened.

Through all of this, no one from the village had awakened. Remus threw a few more sticks on the fire and suggested that we all go back to sleep. He and Nivea would take the first watch as guards, promising to wake Romulus to take the next turn. I could not fall asleep at once, so I stared at the starry sky. Glancing over at Remus and Nivea, I noticed both of them had already fallen asleep. Having confidence in Nivea's judgment, I fell asleep, too.

Chapter V

Lamia did not understand what had happened. A mortal dog, seeming to possess inexplicable powers, had driven her away, denying her the human meal she craved. The frustrated spirit sought advice from Discordia.

"Do not be so dismayed, Lamia," suggested Discordia. "There will be other opportunities to feed on a human. Their good fortune cannot last for long, this I promise you."

The morning sun woke us, and I wondered if I had dreamed the events of the night before. Turning to Chiara, who slept beside me, I asked, "Did Lamia try to steal Nico last night, or did I have a ghastly dream?"

"If it was a dream, then I had it, too."

All of us were a little bewildered by what happened the night before. When we shared our story about Lamia with the villagers who awakened first, they rushed from hut to hut to tell the others. It was not long before the whole village surrounded us, trying to learn every detail of the incident.

"It is no surprise that she chose Nico," insisted Julia. "He is the youngest."

"But how did she know which was the youngest?" I asked. "And how did she manage to come to him without awakening the rest of us?"

"Lamia was once a beautiful woman," said Varro. "She was cursed by the ancient gods and became the shapeshifter you saw last night. She usually preys on young people, but when her hunger is excessive, she will suck the blood of an adult. As an immortal, she could easily appear among you, steal Nico, and be gone without anyone noticing."

"Yet Nivea was able to stop her," said Chiara.

"That I cannot explain," replied Varro. "There is no doubt that Nivea is no ordinary dog. Just look at her, more than fifteen years old, yet she has the boundless energy of a puppy."

"She has been a friend and protector our whole lives," observed Romulus. "Let's hope that her energy doesn't diminish. We have a long way to go until we reach Cumae."

The people of Apia gave us what food they could spare. Their special gift, however, was more specific directions to Cumae.

"There are two roads to the south," said Claudius. "I have traveled each of them to

Tarracina, but not all the way to Cumae." He looked at the map that Massimo had drawn and nodded his head. "Massimo's map is just as I remember the roads. One is farther inland near the foothills of the mountains. The other is closer to the sea."

Varro cautioned us, saying, "Both roads are well-traveled, including by Veiians. We still don't know why they attacked Fontis, but you should be wary. You may want to travel at night, or if you use the road by daylight, be alert for strangers and leave the road when you see them."

"If I were you, I would take the road that is closer to the coast," suggested Claudius. "The inland road is better, and most travelers prefer it. Because we don't know what prompted the attack on your village, the fewer travelers you meet, the better."

It was then that I asked a question that had been bothering me. "How will we find Cumae?" I felt a little foolish asking the question, and I felt much better when the others agreed with me.

"All we know is that Cumae is a great settlement," added Remus.

Smiling, Julia said, "Cumae is more than a great settlement. It is an *urbs*, a city. The buildings are made of stone. Many of them are bigger than anything you have ever seen. It is on the coast beside a huge harbor, and in the distance to the south is Mons Vesuvius, a mountain of fire. Between the stone buildings and the mountain of fire, it will seem as if you are in another world."

"I can help us find the way," blurted Nico proudly. "The sun rose there," he said as he pointed with his left hand. "That means my right hand is toward the west, and I am facing south. We must head toward that distant hill. I'll check the stars each night to be sure we are going the right way."

"Thank you, Nico. Your knowledge will be helpful on this trip," said Romulus. He put his hand on the boy's shoulder fondly. Although he and everyone else in the group knew how to find the directions using the sun during the day and the stars at night, he did not mention this. Romulus and the others accepted Nico's comment graciously, realizing that it was the boy's way of contributing to the task of finding Cumae.

After thanking the people of Apia and saying goodbye to our friends and families, we continued on our journey. We headed west and south toward the sea, for that was the direction of the road we would take toward Cumae. We passed the inland road, which also led to Cumae, but as advised, we did not take it. Our journey took us over several hills that gave us a view of the sea, and it was an awesome sight. It stretched as far as the eye could see and was larger than any of us could have imagined. The biggest body of water any of us had ever seen was the *lacus* near Alba Longa, and it was nothing compared to the sea.

By that afternoon, we reached the road that

would take us south. Because the sun was setting, we decided to find a safe place to spend the night. One of the hills near the road had a group of red rocks just below its summit. Some of the rocks formed an overhang under which we could sleep. It was less secure than a cave, but we could build a fire, and it would not be obvious to travelers on the road. From the rocks, we could see anyone who would approach, and perhaps defend ourselves.

Our experience of the night before made us all anxious. Romulus suggested that three of us at a time should stand watch. When I asked him why not just one at a time so we would all have a chance to sleep decently that night, he grinned and said, "With three guards, at least one of us will be able to wake the other two when they fall asleep, which all of us will." He was right, of course.

Thankfully, the night was peaceful. All of us had a turn standing watch, and as Romulus implied, we struggled to stay awake. His suggestion about having three guards proved to be necessary, and it worked. The only one who had a good night's sleep was Nivea, who slept soundly until dawn.

In the morning, we hurried to get on our way as soon as there was enough light to see. We felt we could travel for a time on the road before the traders started moving. It also seemed unlikely that the Veiians would begin searching for us this early, if they were looking for us. Our breakfast was bread, fruit, and cheese, all of which we could eat while walking.

"We should probably stay in a line with no more than two or three of us together," suggested Remus. "If we stay in a large group, we can easily be surrounded, and we will get in each other's way if we are attacked."

He was right, but what he said made us nervous. Until he spoke, we had forgotten the reason we were traveling and were enjoying the morning. We were now more alert for danger, and we all stayed close to the side of the road.

"How far will we walk today?" asked Nico. He was at the head of the line with Nivea and Romulus. Despite being the youngest, he was determined not to be a burden to the rest of us.

"I think we can make ten *milles* today," answered Romulus. "Have you ever walked that far in a day?"

"Isn't that how far we walked yesterday?"

Romulus could not help but admire Nico. The boy was right of course. Our walk yesterday was probably the same distance he had proposed for today. Soldiers on foot were required to walk fifteen *milles* or more in a day, but that would probably be too much to ask of us. If we had to leave the road very often, it would be impossible.

"We can do more than ten *milles*," said Chiara, who had joined the two of them.

"Maybe, but we have to find food, and that

will take time. We will also have to get off the road soon so we won't be seen." Pausing for a moment, Romulus added, "I have no idea why I am thinking in terms of *milles*. Massimo said that it would take us about ten days, and we have no way of measuring *milles*. I'm not much of a leader, am I?"

Raising her eyebrows, Chiara said, "So far, you have been a great leader. We aren't lost, hungry, or dead."

The sun was high enough in the sky that we began to worry about others seeing us. We did not fear the traders who used the road, but they might tell others that they had seen us, and it could get back to the Veiians. Romulus waved us off the road, and we withdrew into the trees.

Even though the trees were not close together, it was much slower moving among them than on the road. Nivea, however, always seemed to know the best way, no matter how thick the brush or rocky the terrain. It was also Nivea who warned us of the first travelers on the road. She came to a stop, growled, and stared toward the road.

"Everybody down," whispered Remus. "Get behind a tree if you can."

At first we could see nothing, but we heard sounds in the distance. The sounds came from the south and grew louder. When the travelers were beside us on the road, we could see that they were Greeks. Some rode horses, while others walked. Horses pulled carts that were filled with clay pots packed in straw. I recognized a few of the Greeks, and I'm sure the others did, too. None of us said anything, and within a few minutes, their voices had disappeared. We looked at Remus, who signaled with his hand that we should stay down. Only after several minutes did he rise and move toward the road. Seeing no one else, he returned to us, and we resumed our trek.

Some of the trees we passed by had fruit, which we picked and ate or kept for later. With Nivea's help, we even killed a boar. After we dressed it, two of us at a time took turns carrying the boar suspended on a long stick. Although this burden made our journey more difficult, we thought it was better that we keep moving during the day and cook the boar for our evening meal.

The rest of the day was more or less dull, for which we were grateful. We plodded along, checking the road from time to time to be sure we were heading in the right direction. Nico, of course, insisted all along that he had been using landmarks he had established from sunrise, and he was right. At no time did we drift from the road.

A curious thing happened toward nightfall. As the sun was setting, Nivea led us inland away from the coast and the road. At first, we tried to ignore her and stay on the road, but she was insistent, barking and whining to show she disagreed with where we were going.

"She must know what she is doing," insisted Romulus. "In all the years she has been with us, she has never led us the wrong way."

"I really hope she is right this time," whined Nico, who was helping to carry the boar. "Our dinner is getting heavy."

Romulus was right to trust our dog, remarkably so. We went where Nivea led us, and soon came upon a small settlement of just a few huts. At first, we were not sure what to do, but Nivea made that decision easy. She ran toward the huts barking. People came out of the huts and from nearby pastures. We were completely vulnerable and didn't know what to do. The reaction of the people was unexpected and strangely comforting.

The people of the settlement greeted Nivea as if she were an old friend. We stayed where we were until a kind voice said, "Come, you are welcome." Romulus asked us to stay where we were and approached the people of the settlement.

"Thanks for welcoming us. How do you know Nivea?"

"We do not know the dog you call Nivea, but we know her breed. Dogs like her work with shepherds. We are shepherds, and we assumed you were."

"We were shepherds, but we had to leave our home. I am Romulus, and we are going to Cumae."

Feeling confident that the people were

friendly, Romulus waved at us, and we walked toward the huts. One of the men looked at Romulus, Remus, and Nivea and said, "I know who you are. You are the *gemelli*, the twins who were raised by a wolf. But this is not a wolf. She is a herding dog. In any case you are all welcome, especially if you are willing to share that boar."

"The boar is more than we can eat, and we are happy to share it with you," said Remus. "Your cooking fire is already burning, you have plenty of wood, so let's get started."

Some of us helped the villagers prepare the boar, while others told the story of what had happened to us. The people of Pontia—the place was named for a bridge they had built across a stream—were stunned to hear of the attack and the sundering that followed. They were also concerned for their own safety. Veiians often used both roads that went north to south, and their settlement was between them.

The conversation turned away from the problems of the last few days to more pleasant matters. We learned more about Cumae and the Greeks, and we were pleased that the Pontians agreed with our decision to go there. They traded with the Greeks, and they believed that we would find work there and would be allowed to settle nearby.

The boar provided a wonderful meal, and after we had eaten, the Pontians offered to let us share their huts. Although we were at first reluctant to impose on them, Marcus, their leader, pointed to the gathering clouds. "You will have many nights with nasty weather, I am sure. Why not make tonight a pleasant one?" His words convinced us, and we divided ourselves into small groups that spent the night with different families.

Chapter VI

"Why do you want me to make Vesuvius erupt?" asked Vulcanus.

"No special reason," insisted Discordia, although she knew exactly why she wanted an eruption. "I simply enjoy seeing how powerful you are and experiencing the beauty of your fire from within Earth. But there is no hurry. We can talk again."

Although he was always suspicious of Discordia, Vulcanus was also flattered by her attention. Perhaps he would agree to her request.

For the next eight days, we made our way toward Cumae. We traveled mostly at night and used the road sparingly. It rained several times, and we were miserable. During the storms, we thought of Marcus, his good advice, and the night we spent in Pontia inside the huts instead of outside in the rain. As before, Nivea led us, although we often questioned her judgment. She took us through rugged hills and valleys when it seemed to us much more sensible to stay close to the road. We saw occasional parties of travelers on the road, so her instincts seemed to be correct.

Traveling at night had a benefit we had not anticipated. We were more relaxed napping during the day, when it was a little warmer and we were less fearful of Lamia. Although she never came back, her image still haunted us.

About halfway through our journey, we came upon a swamp called the Pomptinus Ager. All of us knew the stories of the swamp, which was supposed to be the home of the goddess Febris. Unlike most immortals, whose actions are often predictable, Febris could be either benevolent or dangerous. She could infect you with a fever that might kill you, or spare you, depending on her mood. No one was sure how the fever was spread, but it often seemed to come from swampy areas where a small, buzzing insect called *musca* lived in great numbers. These insects landed on the skin of a human or animal and fed on blood, leaving behind an itchy bump.

Nivea led us well inland and away from the swamp, and Febris spared us. Fever was not the only peril we faced, however. On a hill overlooking the swamp was Tarracina, an Etruscan town. The people of Tarquinii founded Tarracina, and they are allied with Veii. To skirt the settlement without being seen, we had to undertake the most difficult part of our journey and climb a rocky ridge at night.

Passing Tarracina and the swamp safely was important because it marked the halfway point of our journey. After that, things were a little easier because we knew we were getting closer to Cumae. We were less worried about being seen by the Veiians or their allies. The two main roads joined and headed inland, while we stayed close to the shoreline.

Early one morning, as the fog was lifting, Chiara shouted, "Look, that mountain in the distance. It must be Vesuvius. We can't be far from Cumae!"

All of us strained to see what she was talking about. The fog made it difficult to see, but eventually we made out a mountain that seemed to have two peaks, one being slightly higher than the other. No other mountains were anywhere near as tall as they were, so Chiara was probably right. Our journey was coming to an end, and Cumae was not far ahead.

"According to the map, we will be able to reach Cumae by *nona hora*, the middle of the day," said Remus. "We still must be cautious, however. The Etruscans trade with the Greeks."

"What we might do is walk around Cumae and approach the city from the south," said Chiara. "I think most of the roads come to Cumae from the north, and that is the direction that the Veiians and other Etruscans would be traveling."

Her suggestion made sense, although it made our journey longer. We would have to go around Cumae and head inland. The terrain was hilly, but we felt that was an advantage, because traders would be less likely to pass nearby. In addition, we kept the hills between Cumae and us, which added to our cover. Romulus would sometimes climb to the top of one of the hills to look for Cumae and keep us oriented.

As we turned back toward Cumae from the south, we experienced some worrisome happenings. A few clouds drifted above Vesuvius, but there was no fire coming from the mountain. The ground between Vesuvius and us was smoking, however. In the distance, we could see pools of water that seemed to be boiling, and we could smell something terrible.

"They say an entrance to the Underworld is here," whispered Chiara. "I never believed it, but I do now. When my parents told me the stories, I thought they were making it all up."

"No one could make this up," insisted Romulus. "I can't imagine why the Greeks chose to settle here."

"They didn't come here first," said Chiara. "Their first colony was on the island of Pithecusa, not far from here. You can see it in the distance. They came here later. The Greeks have made cities all around the sea."

All of us wanted to be there as soon as we could. Although we were tired after a long journey, we made good time. When we reached high ground close enough to see the settlement, we were astounded. Cumae was larger than any village we had ever seen, and some of the buildings were made of stone.

To no one in particular, I sighed, "The Greeks must be the finest builders on Earth."

"And this is one of their smaller towns," said Chiara. "The traders insist the most elegant cities are across the sea in their homeland."

"Chiara, you know more Greek than most of us. I know just a little. Maybe you and I should go to Cumae and let the others wait here," suggested Romulus.

Nodding her head, Chiara answered. "I think you are right. It might be worrisome to them to see this many strangers."

The two of them walked to the edge of Cumae with Nivea at their side. Several men on horseback greeted them. One of the riders dismounted and started talking to them enthusiastically. We could barely hear what they said, but the man seemed to recognize both of them, especially Chiara.

"Chiara, what are you doing here so far from your village?" asked the rider. He was about the same age we were.

"It's a long story, but I am very happy to see you, Milo. We need your help. This is my cousin Romulus."

Holding out his hand in friendship to

Romulus, Milo commented, "I thought I recognized your face. You come from a village near Chiara. You are one of the *gemelli*, and this is your herding dog."

"Yes, Milo, and I remember you. We'll explain everything, but can we have the rest of the group join us? We didn't want to frighten anybody by marching in with the whole group."

"Of course. Your people are always welcome here, and I want to hear the story. I don't know your plan, but you will spend the night with us, won't you?"

The three of them waved, and we hurried to join them, relieved that things had gone so well. Even though we had traded with the Greeks, we were not their allies, and they traded with the Etruscans. We also felt more at ease putting distance between the fiery ground and us.

The two riders who had been with Milo hurried back to the settlement. Milo went with us into Cumae. By the time we arrived, people had gathered, believing that we were there to trade. They spoke among themselves in Greek, and although I did not understand all of what they said, I could guess what they were talking about. We were just teenagers, and we carried nothing of value to trade.

The leader of Cumae was Antenor, who was Milo's uncle. He and several elders met us, and we told our story to them and the others who had assembled. Chiara and Milo interpreted back and forth between Latin, our language, and Greek. It was not an easy task, but the people of Cumae seemed to understand what happened, specifically the sundering, because it was one of their ancestral stories.

They found the attack of the Veiians troubling. The Greeks traded with all the Etruscan tribes, but they were still outsiders. The Etruscans valued their goods, but there was tension between them. The Greeks were clearly a strong power, with ships, weapons, and fighting men. They had a notable reputation among the other trading nations.

The Etruscans, in contrast, were a rising power. They were a confederation of city-states that spoke the same language and shared customs. They were not yet a seafaring nation like the Greeks, but they controlled much of the peninsula of land that stretched into the sea. They had resources like iron and copper that were valued by the Greeks, and they were eager to obtain goods made by the Greeks. The Etruscans learned much from the Greeks, but they were also a bit envious and might someday challenge them.

"So you left home with nothing except your clothes and a little food?" asked Antenor. "That's very courageous. Some might even call it foolish. Even the Lydians had more than that when their sundering took place."

"We were not afraid or foolish," mumbled Nico. "Our parents gave each of us one of our

Lares." Reaching into his tunic, he pulled out a small statue of his family's household god. "And we have Nivea to guide us. She is the best dog in the world."

Some of us, myself among them, felt that Nico's words might be misunderstood by Antenor and the other Greeks. Their reaction, however, was very unexpected. They nodded their heads and smiled at one another.

"In our history, another person fled with little other than the images of his gods. Aeneas, after enabling the escape of the elders, women, and children from Troy, left with a small band of warriors. They carried their weapons and the images of their gods, many of whom we shared. The Greeks recognized their courage and the way they honored the gods, so they let them pass. Some say that Aeneas and his followers came to this land, so perhaps he is your ancestor. Given these circumstances, the very least we can do is show you hospitality."

Antenor then asked the question that took the conversation in a new direction. "Now that you have been forced to leave your home, what are your plans?"

We looked at each other, but no one spoke immediately. Romulus turned to Chiara and nodded his head. Because she was the best speaker of Greek, he wanted her to explain what we hoped for.

"The Greeks have always been good to us.

You have traded fairly and taught us much. We hoped that there might be work for us here. If we show how hard we can work, you would accept us into your settlement. All of us have worked beside our families in the fields, and some of us have special skills that will help you."

A silence fell over the group as we awaited an answer. Then a farmer said, "I need help right away with the harvest and can use several workers. I am willing to pay a share of my crops and provide a living space. It is not much more than a shed, but it is clean and has a place for a fire."

Almost at once, all the others expressed a need for help. Potters, metal workers, farmers, and builders all came forward. The success of the Greeks as traders and growers had produced a shortage of labor because it took so long to travel from their homeland to this colony. The arrival of experienced workers was most welcome, even though we were fairly young.

The joy we felt was extraordinary, and we forgot for a moment the circumstances that brought us here. No one was more expressive than Chiara, who hugged Milo enthusiastically. It became clear to all of us why her Greek was so good, and why Milo visited Apia so often.

While this was going on, I saw something that changed my life forever. Not far from Antenor sat a man at a simple table. On the table was a piece of animal skin, and the man was making marks with what looked like a sliver of bone or the shaft of a feather. Pulling Chiara away from Milo, I asked what the man was doing.

"It's called writing. Milo explained it to me before. The marks the *scriptor* is making on the animal skin record our words. His writing will help us remember the events that took place today. When people who were not here look at his words, they will know what happened."

Chiara's words were baffling to me. All of our stories were told from one person to another. Sometimes we drew pictures, but the details of the stories were always given by word of mouth. Our history, our family stories, and our legends were exchanged by word of mouth. It had always been this way.

I walked over to the man and watched him making marks on the animal skin. I could make no sense of them at all. They were written neatly in lines across the skin, and some of the symbols were repeated. The man looked up at me and spoke in Latin.

"Have you never seen writing before?"

"No, I have never seen writing before, and I'm not sure I understand how it works." I hesitated as I spoke, feeling a little embarrassed.

"Your curiosity is a good thing. It is how we learn. My name is Thalis. I am the *scriptor* of Cumae."

"My name is Serena of Fontis. My brothers are Romulus and Remus, the *gemelli*. Please, tell me how your writing works. It looks so magical I can't believe it."

"There are symbols or letters for each sound of our language. You seem to know Milo. Here is his name written in our language." Thalis pointed at several symbols together. He then pointed to another group of symbols. "This group of symbols forms the word *strangers*, which is what I called you, as I know nothing about you and your friends. But now that I know your name, I can write it in our language."

Bending down, he made some marks in the dirt with his finger. "That is Serena. Why don't you trace your name with your finger?"

I dropped to my knees and traced over the symbols. Thalis guided me so I made the strokes of the symbols in the same order as he did. When I finished, I felt a thrill and could not help but stare at my name in the dirt. Then a thought struck me.

"But doesn't it take a long time to write stories about people and events? Isn't it easier just to tell the story with spoken words?" I asked.

"Of course you are right," answered Thalis, "but once spoken, words are gone. The story must be retold as many times as someone wants to hear it. With each retelling, something might be lost or changed. When we write a story on parchment, however, the words last a long time. Many people can share them. This animal skin can be sent to Greece so the people there know what we are doing so far from home. The work of writing might be hard, but the result is knowledge that can live forever."

Chapter VII

"The entrance to the Underworld has been opened," said Vulcanus. "Are you satisfied?"

"I am grateful," answered Discordia, "but see how the humans respond. They are hardly troubled by what you have done. Could you not show them more of your power?"

Vulcanus thought about what Discordia had said. He had no issue with the humans, but she was right. The Greeks had become accustomed to the occasional activity of Vesuvius. Perhaps it was time to show them a little more of his power.

The words that Thalis spoke had an enormous effect on me. What he said made perfect sense. Writing might require effort, but it was a precious art. Knowledge and stories could be shared across time and distance as never before. I did not understand the symbols he made, but they had a certain kind of beauty. Some day, I promised myself, I would learn to write in our language.

My thoughts were interrupted in a most unnerving way. The ground began to tremble, just a little at first, and then more violently. As terrifying as it was, what took place afterward was even more awful. Plumes of smoke rose from Vesuvius, and within minutes, they had become billowing clouds. Flames shot forth from the crest of the mountain, and lightning flashed among the clouds.

Although we were in a state of panic, the Greeks were not very troubled. "We have seen Vesuvius come to life before," insisted Milo. "We are too far away to be affected. Events like this come to nothing."

I cannot begin to describe how I felt, and I am sure the others were just as uneasy. This was the most frightening incident of my life, worse than the attack of the Veiians. A story we thought was just a legend proved once again to be true. Vesuvius was indeed a gateway to the Underworld.

Although we hoped Milo's complacence was deserved, in this instance he was mistaken. Not only did the explosions from Vesuvius continue, but the burning fields near Cumae also became more active. Great cracks opened up in the ground, and from them came geysers of foul-smelling liquids. The seething pools released gases that were repugnant beyond description. Breathing became harder, and the temperature got hotter.

The shaking increased, people were knocked down, and buildings collapsed. Clouds from Vesuvius drifted in the wind toward us, and within a short time, flakes of ash began falling from the sky. Although we were far from the mountain, we could see fiery molten rock oozing from the top and moving down the side of the mountain.

All of us were paralyzed, not knowing what to do. Even the Greeks were at a loss. It was Nivea who saved us. She howled, looked at us, and ran west toward the sea. We followed her at once, and after a moment's hesitation, so did the Greeks.

Reaching the shore, we began to board the boats, along with the Greeks. I had never been on a boat before, but I had seen them on the lake near our home. Although I felt fearful being in a boat on the sea, I was even more frightened of what was happening on the land.

It was then that we became concerned about Nivea. She was nowhere to be seen. Romulus and Remus jumped off the boat they had boarded and ran around searching for her. Looking back toward Cumae, they saw her heading toward an opening in a hillside.

"It is the cave of the Sibyl, the prophetess who tells the future," said Milo. "In our fear, we forgot completely about her. Thank the gods for Nivea. Had the Sibyl been lost, who knows what would have become of us."

The three of them ran toward the cave, and

for the moment, the rain of ash stopped. They entered the cave and came out shortly leading the oracle. They guided the seemingly frail woman to the boats with Nivea close behind. While the drama of the rescue of the Sibyl took place, not a single boat pushed off from shore.

When they reached the safety of the shoreline and climbed into a boat, the eruption resumed even more powerfully than before. The rain of ash was replaced with small pellets—lapilli—falling from the sky. The storm of rocks was more intense over the land, but we could see that the nearby sea was undisturbed. Fearing damage to the sails, Antenor shouted orders that they should not be raised, and that we should row toward open water. Everyone who was able grabbed an oar. We had never rowed a boat, but by watching the others and imitating what they did, we managed to be helpful.

Once we reached open water, we were beyond the rain of lapilli. The crew of Antenor's boat raised its sail, and he signaled that the others should do the same. With the wind at our back, we headed toward an island that was not far away.

Both the Sibyl and Nivea were on our boat. The dog sat by the oracle with her head on the woman's lap. Although they had never encountered one another before, at least to our knowledge, they seemed to be old friends. The Sibyl spoke to Nivea and bent over the dog as if she were listening for a response. My curiosity about this was interrupted by my brother's voice.

"That must be Pithecusa," said Romulus, who sat near me. "Chiara said that the Greeks had a settlement there. I don't think the ash or lava from Vesuvius will reach the island."

"Our village on Pithecusa is not very large," added Milo. "It is more like a trading port. There are no farms or places where metal is worked or pots are made. But I think we will be safe there."

As we drew near to the island, however, we saw a troubling sight. Ships were rowing away from the island toward us. Antenor's boat stopped and dropped its anchor, and the other boats drew near it. The people from the island joined us, and their news was not good. The small volcano on the island was coming to life. From where we were, we could see clouds of smoke rising from its summit.

Speaking loudly from his boat, Antenor said to all of us, "We have few choices. Because we left so quickly, we have no supplies for a long voyage. The volcanoes are preventing us from returning to Cumae or Pithecusa. Maybe we can sail north close to the shore but beyond the rain of ash."

Hearing his words, the Sibyl rose to her feet. In a surprisingly strong voice she said, "There is no need to sail north. The eruption will soon be over. When it is, most of us can return to Cumae or Pithecusa, but not the young people of Fontis. Their future is elsewhere. They should all board the boat with Milo and his sailors and follow the prevailing wind. There will be a sign that they will recognize when they have reached their destination."

To the Greeks, the words of the Sibyl were like commands. To us, they made little sense. Who could know when a volcano would stop? Why weren't we allowed to return to the mainland? What sign should we look for? We had no experience with the Sibyl, although we had heard stories of her prophecies. I turned to my brothers and friends, and all of them had a look of dejection on their faces. The hope we had felt upon reaching Cumae had vanished, only to be replaced by despair.

Most of us were already on Milo's boat. The boats carrying the others maneuvered beside us and exchanged passengers. Even before the process was completed, however, the noise from Vesuvius was subsiding. The flames were no longer visible, and the plumes of smoke and ash diminished.

The Sibyl was the last to leave our boat. She stroked Nivea several times and then spoke to us. "Your fate is in the hands of the gods, but you are not powerless. You will face many challenges, and the brothers who have led you this far will not fail you. Nor will Nivea. A special destiny awaits you."

Heeding the advice of the Sibyl, Milo and his men raised the sail, which they had dropped while the boats were gathered together. The wind filled the sail and drove us south. We watched the other boats heading to their original ports, now that the volcanoes were no longer active.

"If we continue to sail in this direction, what is the first significant landfall?" asked Remus.

"The island of Sicania is southwest of us," answered Milo. "It is about two days of sailing. Our people have towns there. None are very large, but they all have farms. The land is very fertile, and the weather is good. We will pass a few smaller islands on the way, but they have little to offer us, other than sea birds."

"Do we have enough food and water for two days?" wondered Romulus.

"No, but we can put into shore before nightfall. Some streams flow into the ocean, there are fruit trees in the area, and we can hunt small animals. The fishing is also good along the coast. The Sibyl did not forbid us from stopping to acquire supplies. She just said that we should follow the prevailing wind."

"What about that place?" asked Chiara, pointing to an island between the boat and the mainland.

"That is the Island of the Wild Boars, a beautiful place where some of our people live now. It would indeed be fortunate if the wind changed direction and brought us there, but I doubt that an island so close to home is what the Sibyl had in mind," answered Milo. "There is something else to consider. The island has no springs or streams, so the people who live there catch rainwater in cisterns. They do not have enough to share with us."

Milo steered the ship toward the mainland, carefully avoiding some rocky islands on the way. He and his sailors watched the islands fearfully; at least that is what I thought. I was not alone.

"Are you expecting trouble?" asked Romulus. "You seem a little worried."

"Those islands are the Sirenuse, and they used to be the home of the Sirens. These creatures were half bird and half woman. They lured sailors to the islands with beautiful songs, where the waves dashed their boats upon the rocks. It was Odysseus who caused them to die. He sailed this way after the war with Troy. Knowing the story of the sirens, he had his men fill their ears with wax so they would not hear the song. On his orders, the sailors tied him to the mast. As they sailed past, hearing the songs almost drove Odysseus mad. But his men heard nothing and would not turn toward the islands. Because a human was able to ignore their songs, the Sirens cast themselves into the sea and died. Even so, we are always cautious when we sail by the islands."

The rocky shoreline was beautiful to behold, but it seemed too steep for us to land safely. The cliffs were almost vertical, with nothing but rocks at their base. Thankfully, Milo did not attempt to land at this spot. Instead, he let the wind drive us south past an outcropping of rocks. As if by magic, a beach appeared at the base of the cliffs.

Milo steered the boat close to the shore while his men lowered the sails and dropped the anchor. Two sailors jumped into the water and swam to shore holding ropes. When they were firmly on shore, the anchor was lifted and the men pulled the boat onto the beach.

"Why didn't you just land on the beach?" asked Remus.

"I'm not that familiar with this spot," replied Milo, "but from others who have been here, I thought it was fairly safe. I didn't know if there were rocks just under the surface of the water. We use this technique when we land in new places."

The sun was low in the western sky when we left the boat. The beach was not light-colored sand, as were the beaches farther north. It was black and made of tiny stones rounded by the action of the sea. I couldn't help but pick up some of the stones. They were smooth and beautiful, many having streaks of white. At another time, I might have wandered the beach admiring them.

Beyond the beach were steep cliffs covered with vegetation. A few caves dotted the cliffs. Living here would be hard, for there was almost no place to graze animals or grow vegetables. The land would be easy to defend, however. No attacker could come unnoticed.

Milo sent some of us to the stream to get water and collect fruit if we could find it. Others took nets or spears and tried to catch some fish. Milo and several of his men built a fire on the beach from driftwood. Their weapons were nearby, but they had no reason to use them. The people who lived in the caves and stone dwellings on the cliffs high must have seen our landing, but they paid no attention to us.

After stocking the boat with water and fruit for the journey, we ate the fish that the men had caught. It was a meager meal, but we were grateful. Sitting by the fire, we talked about the day and what tomorrow would bring. Although we knew that we would probably be safer spending the night in the boat close to shore, we decided to sleep by the fire. None of us knew how long we would be sailing, and the fire seemed especially comforting after an unimaginable day.

Chapter VIII

"They think they have escaped," murmured Discordia to the Keres, "but they have only postponed the inevitable. I will have all of them suffer, including the Greeks."

Staring at the sea far below her, Discordia held her hand out and whispered, "Karybdis, I implore you to help me. A Greek ship has defied you. If you would swallow the ship, I would be forever in your debt."

On the bottom of the sea, a horrid being stirred, pleased that a goddess had remembered her. The shapeless monster opened her great mouth to suck in the water and anything that floated on it.

In the morning, we set off soon after waking. The sun was just rising, and because of the mountains behind the beach, we were still in the darkness just before dawn. As the sky brightened, the sea became more beautiful, changing from gray to shades of blue.

Most of us boarded the boat and prepared to pull the oars. Two sailors pushed the prow of the boat off the beach. Once they had climbed on board, Milo signaled us, and we began to row. When he was confident we were clear of underwater rocks, he raised the sail. There was not much of a breeze, so we made little progress. Even so, Milo did not want us to row until we were exhausted. It was better, he said, to save our strength, not knowing what was ahead of us.

"Tell us about the place we are heading," suggested Romulus.

Milo held the tiller of the boat and described the island. "We call the island Sicania, and it is part of *Magna Graecia*, Great Greece, which includes parts of the island and the mainland on which you live. We have settled along the coast, and there are other people who live there. We have begun building cities, but most of our people there are farmers, fishermen, or sea traders."

Looking back at Vesuvius, which he could see in the distance, he added, "The land itself is beautiful, a mix of fertile plains, hills, and mountains. One of the mountains is a fiery giant like Vesuvius. Some people believe it is the home of Cyclopes, the one eyed monster. Others think that Zeus buried Enceladus there after he and the other giants challenged the Olympians."

Hearing his words, we all turned to look at Vesuvius. The mountain was quiet and stood as a lonely sentinel beside the bay. A few wisps of smoke drifted from its peak, but otherwise, it was silent.

Seeing our unease, Milo said, "Etna, as we call the fiery mountain, is friendlier than Vesuvius. It rarely explodes, and it gives us warning when it does. The native inhabitants of Sicania are not afraid of the mountain, but they don't live on its slopes. Our settlements are far from the mountain."

The wind freshened, and the boat picked up speed. We were still heading more or less south, but Milo had steered us away from the coast. In the deeper water, we were less likely to encounter underwater reefs. He said that at this speed, we might even reach Sicania by morning. In spite of the harrowing events of the day before, things at last seemed to be going well.

Remus and Chiara sat in the stern of the boat and made small talk with Milo while he steered. Romulus stood on the prow of the boat looking at the sea with Nivea at his side. He seemed more relaxed than I had seen him in days. That made what came next all the more disturbing. His face, which had been peaceful, assumed a look of concern. His eyes focused on the sea just ahead of us.

"Milo, drop the sail and turn sharply in any direction. Then get up here and look at this.

Something terrible is in front of us."

All of us who were sitting quickly rose to our feet and looked at the sea ahead of us. A whirlpool had formed out of nowhere, and our boat was slowly being drawn into it. What was worse, the spinning water was moving faster, and the whirlpool was growing larger.

Some of the Greek sailors immediately dropped the sail, and Milo pulled the tiller to turn the boat. It was too late. We had been caught in the swirling waters and were drifting sideways closer to the vortex.

"It's that cursed Karybdis," muttered Milo. "She has been devouring ships since humans set sail upon the seas. One of the gods must be angry with us."

"What can we do?" asked Remus, who was as unfamiliar with the sea as the rest of us. We had never heard of Karybdis, although we had been told stories of dangerous whirlpools forming in the sea.

"To the oars, everyone," ordered Milo. "If we can turn away from the whirlpool and catch the wind, we might be able to sail around it."

But by then we were closer to the center of the whirlpool, and the oars had no effect. Some of the oars could not even reach the water because the boat was tilting at a sharp angle. The craft spun around helplessly, and we were being drawn into the bottomless hole at the center of the vortex. There was no escape.

While we pulled at the oars, Nivea walked back and forth in the boat howling. It was the same sound she made when she found wandering sheep and wanted help to drive them back to the flock. None of us was in a position to calm her down, even though her cries went unanswered. Or so we thought.

The moment Nivea stopped howling, Remus let go of his oar and stood up. Pointing between the boat and the center of the vortex, he cried out loudly enough to be heard above the roaring of the water, "We are surely doomed. Karybdis is not alone. A sea serpent has arisen from the whirlpool."

When we looked to where he was pointing, we saw something that defied belief. Between the vortex and us was a giant sea serpent of the kind known only in legends. Its head was larger than our boat and rose out of the water higher than the mast. Covered with green scales, the beast would have been a beautiful sight to behold, had it not been intent on destroying us. All of us stopped and stared, knowing that our end was near.

In the prow of the boat, Nivea looked into the eyes of the sea serpent. She made the quiet noises of a dog seeing an old friend after a long separation. The sea serpent drew near and lowered its head. As gently as possible for a beast of that size, it nudged our boat away from the whirlpool. The serpent was not affected by the whirlpool, and it disrupted the swirling water so we were no longer spinning. With each movement of its head, we drifted farther from the vortex, eventually reaching calm water.

The sea serpent saw that we were out of danger and ceased pushing us. For a moment, it looked at Nivea before raising its head skyward. An eerie yet beautiful sound came from the leviathan at the same time that Nivea began to howl. The music they made together was indescribable. Nodding its head, the sea serpent withdrew into the depths.

Nivea turned and wagged her tail as if nothing unusual had happened. Romulus knelt beside her and put his arms around her neck. Remus said, "Nivea, there is something about you that we don't understand. I hope that some day we learn your secret."

Awed by what he saw but knowing that we were still not far from the whirlpool, Milo ordered his men to raise the sail. Favorable winds blew us north, which we agreed was a mixed blessing. We were sailing farther away from Karybdis, but we were heading in the direction from which we had just come. It was Romulus who reminded us that the Sibyl did not tell us the direction we should be going, only that we should follow the prevailing wind.

We retraced the route we had just taken, although we were farther out to sea. The beach where we had spent the night came into view, as did the islands of the Sirens. Later in the day, we passed the Island of the Wild Boars.

The wind kept us away from the mainland, which was something that worried us. Milo was not bothered, as he had spent most of his life sailing. He explained that the weather was good, we had food and water, and it would not be a problem spending the night at sea. The moon would be almost full, and he and his sailors would find a shallow spot to drop anchor.

"There are some small islands in this direction," Milo explained. "One of them is Tyrrhenia. Some believe it or a neighboring island is the home of the sorceress, Circe. I have heard the stories, but I do not believe them. The island is covered with giant trees, some of the largest I have ever seen. Not many people live on the island, and if we end up there, they will undoubtedly flee from where we land."

"Is that where you would like to go?" asked Romulus.

Milo answered with a little embarrassment. "I don't have any idea where it is, or for that matter, where any of the other islands are. I've never come at the islands from this direction. We normally sail along the coast. Once we have our bearings based on landmarks, we head west. Our major landmarks here are the Island of the Wild Boars and Vesuvius, which we can see behind us. The others can't be seen from where we are. We will do as the Sibyl suggested and let the wind guide us. We know where the mainland is, so if any problems arise, we can steer in that direction."

The sunset was glorious, all the more so because we were on the water. We could not help but stare at *sol* as it slowly descended beyond the horizon. With no land to the west and a cloudless sky, we had little perspective with which to judge distances. I reached my hand out, thinking that I might actually touch the sun.

"Darkness will come quickly," said Milo, "so find a comfortable place to sleep. Stay close together to share your body heat. The food and water are in the pots lashed against the side of the boat. Eat and drink enough to maintain your strength, but not too much. We have to ration our food and water. We can head back to the mainland, if necessary, and we may come close enough to an island to get more."

Throughout the night, we took turns sharing the watch with Milo and his men. We thought it was the least we could do, given all that they had gone through because of us. We knew little about the sea or sailing, so we would not have been much use had something happened. Fortunately, nothing out of the ordinary took place.

My brothers and I decided to do our time as lookouts together. The moon and the stars were spectacular. There was no wind, and the sea was quiet. Romulus turned to Milo and said, "You and your men will have our gratitude forever. You willingly put your lives at risk—and continue to do so—for a group of strangers you barely know. I hope that some day we can repay your kindness."

"You are hardly strangers," answered Milo. "Our legends suggest that we might have the same ancestors. You treated us well when we visited your villages. We share the same gods. The Sibyl said that we should deliver you to where the wind leads us. We are bound together in many ways, and if all goes well with Chiara, maybe we will be family some day."

Nico, who was standing at the side of the boat, pointed at the water and whispered *luminosus*. Following his gaze, we saw a sight I shall remember for always. The sea became alive with lights from underwater creatures that shimmered in the waves. We had no idea what they were, but Milo said he had heard legends of the Nereids, the sea nymphs. He had never seen them before.

"Perhaps this is a sign that our fortunes have changed," said Romulus, "and that Neptune, the god of the sea, is sharing a gift with all of us."

Chapter IX

The goddess Carmenta was one of the lesser deities on Olympus. Nonetheless, she took an interest in what was happening with the small group of young people who were making their way across the sea with the help of the Greeks. They had honored her, the goddess of prophecy, by saving the Sibyl and obeying her directions diligently.

"Their story is one for the ages," she thought, "but they have no way to pass it on. I have a special gift for them, letters that they can use to write their own words."

For all of that night and the next morning, the wind blew us north. Around midday, the direction of the wind changed, and we headed east. Milo seemed relieved because we were going toward land, and I must confess that we shared his opinion. None of us had ever spent this much time on a boat, and we were not accustomed to the cramped and difficult conditions on board.

As soon as we spotted land, Romulus asked, "Do you recognize where we are, Milo? Nothing looks familiar to me."

"Those are the Tolfa Mountains," answered Milo. "North of them is the port of Martanum and the Marta River. The people of Martanum provide us with iron in exchange for pottery, gold, and jewelry. We will introduce you to our trading partners."

Unlike our last landing, Milo steered the boat onto the beach near the north bank of the Marta River. He had been here often and knew the area well. A few huts were on some high ground beyond the beach, and a village was not far away. Milo was the first to leave the boat, along with two of his men. No sooner was he on the beach than several people walked down from the huts.

"Milo, we did not expect you so soon, but as always, you are welcome."

"Greetings, Pesna. It is good to see you my friend. I hope all has been well with you. I have a great favor to ask. But first, let me introduce you to our companions."

Milo turned to the boat and waved us onto the beach. We clambered down as he and the Martani approached us.

It is worth mentioning here that none of us had an easy time understanding the conversation. Three languages were in play: Greek, Etruscan, and Latin. Milo was the most capable in all three languages, and I was surprised at Chiara's knowledge. She helped us understand much of what was said. Most of us knew some Etruscan, and Pesna could speak some Latin as well as Greek. In writing this story, I have the benefit of hindsight and the memories of others who were there, which is why I knew what was said.

"These friends are from Fontis, near Alba Longa," explained Milo. "They came to us looking for work, and we welcomed them. Unfortunately, Vesuvius rumbled to life, and we had to flee. There is more to the story, which I shall explain later. What is most important is that the Sibyl said we should follow the wind, and it brought us here."

Pesna looked at us and exclaimed, "They could not have come at a better time. We are in the middle of the harvest season. Coming from the region of Alba Longa, they must be acquainted with gathering crops and herding animals. They will free some of the men who can work in the mines."

Stepping forward, Romulus said, "Thank you, Pesna. I am Romulus, and you are correct. All of us have helped in the fields and orchards. Nivea is an excellent herding dog, and you can count on us to work hard. All we ask is to be treated fairly."

"And you shall. We will offer you a share of this year's crops. Whatever you earn that exceeds your needs can be traded for goods with our neighbors, the Greeks, or us. For now, I am sure I can find families that will house you. If you would like to build your own huts before winter, there is an area at the edge of our village that you may use."

"Milo said that you work iron here. Is there a chance that some of us could learn how to do it?" asked Remus.

"Certainly," answered Pesna, "but the work is not easy. You seem like an eager group, and we have much to do. Come, let's go to the village."

As we walked, Pesna brought up the Arroni, a tribe that lived in the area north of the village. He described them as people from the east who were not associated with any of the Etruscan towns. There had been some raids by the Arroni, but they were more like acts of thievery than the beginning of a war.

"We are partners of a sort with Tarquinii, which is not far from here. All of the villages in the region are part of a central town. Most of us speak the same language. If the Arroni were to attack in force, we could call on the people of Tarquinii and the other villages for assistance."

As Pesna had indicated, the people of Martanum welcomed us, chiefly because we were viewed as capable workers. The town had become very successful because it was a center of trade, was in an agricultural area, and was close to the mines of the Tolfa Mountains. In short, there was more work than there were people, so we were a valuable resource.

We spent the night with generous families. By the next day, we were all working at tasks we had learned at home, picking the crops and helping with the animals. The work was hard, but it was a relief to be in a routine. As the days passed, there was even time for us to build simple shelters at the edge of the village in the style of the Etruscans. Wooden posts held up beams and a conical roof of straw. For now, the walls were sticks lashed to the posts and beams. In time, we would cover the walls with mud.

Milo remained with us for a few days. He and his men helped with the construction of our shelters. He appeared to be negotiating some upcoming trades with the Martani, as he had nothing to exchange now. I am sure that was not the main reason for his staying. His fondness for Chiara became more evident, although they insisted they were nothing more than friends. I wasn't alone in noting this. When the time came for Milo to leave, Romulus made a suggestion that stunned everyone.

"Chiara, my cousin, I have a favor to ask of you. Would you be willing to return to Cumae with Milo? From there, you can make your way back to Fontis to tell our people where we are. Milo may even choose to stop at Ostia and escort you to our village. He probably has friends there who might be heading toward our village anyway."

An awkward silence made everyone feel awkward for a moment. Realizing what Romulus was suggesting, I added, "Please, I know this is an imposition on both of you, but it would bring comfort to our families to know that we are safe and have found a place to settle. And you can return and join us later. You know where we are, and it isn't a difficult journey to get here. Pesna says that there is a good road between here and Alba Longa. The trip is only a few days."

"I'd be really happy to have Chiara with us on our return," said Milo. "I promise to escort her safely back to her village and yours. I would even join her if she decided to come back here."

All of us, including Chiara, knew that Milo was implying a proposal of marriage, but no one said anything about it. Chiara was at the age when most women were married, and she was unquestionably attracted to Milo. Her parents and others from her village knew him because of their trading, and her parents would approve of the marriage. We were all confident that the next time we saw them, it would be as husband and wife.

Chiara agreed to the plan, although she was reluctant to leave us. We assured her that everything would be fine, and that the most vital thing she could do would be to inform our families. The matter was settled, and she left with Milo.

Over the next few days, we learned something

that was new to all of us. We worked for the Martani to earn food, clothes, building material, and such. But we were not paid immediately. We received some goods at once, but some of the payment would be made later. The Martani showed us how they would keep a record of our work and what we would be paid.

At first, it was very confusing and involved writing and numbers. We had no idea what they were doing. It took much explaining by Pesna, but Romulus finally understood and described it to us in our language.

The work we did was written down at the end of each day. The payment we were to receive was also written. Some of it was given to us at once, and the rest of it at a later time. All of this was done with writing and numbers in the Etruscan language on pieces of sheepskin. The process was complicated, but I soon began to understand it. When they wrote the word for *cow*, it meant that we were entitled to a cow at a time in the future. This promise was enforced by Pesna and the other leaders.

The practice of making and keeping promises of trade was nothing new to us, but writing these promises using words and numbers was brilliant. Writing was useful not just for recording stories, as had happened when we arrived at Cumae. It could also be used to ensure the fairness of trade.

Over the next few days, while the others were working in the fields or with the animals, I spent time with Pesna. He showed me how the Etruscan language was written. Each sound had a symbol. The symbols of the Etruscan language were different from those of the Greeks, which I had seen in Cumae.

As I watched him write, I felt a sense of urgency, as if an outside force was prompting me. Our language needed symbols too. When I mentioned this to Pesna, he thought that the Greek or Etruscan symbols would work fine. He and I tried to write our words with these symbols, but our first effort wasn't very good. At that point, Pesna agreed with me that perhaps the Greek or Etruscan symbols were not right for our language.

Pesna suggested something interesting. He and I called together all of us who spoke Latin and several Martani who were good writers. We explained that we were trying to create symbols for the Latin language, just as there were symbols for Greek and Etruscan.

Explaining what we were doing was not easy. Those from Fontis had no idea what writing was supposed to do. Romulus, however, came up with an explanation that made sense.

"Think of stories told with pictures," he said. "There are caves near our home with such stories. Now, instead of drawing a picture of a dog, like Nivea, suppose we had a symbol for her. We could tell a story about Nivea, as long as people knew the symbol."

"But why not just use pictures?" asked Nico.

Romulus considered Nico's suggestion for a moment and then answered. "Some stories can be told with just pictures. But what about feelings like fear when Lamia tried to kidnap you and the bravery of Nivea who saved you? These ideas are hard to explain with just pictures. I think that people will always tell some stories with pictures, but writing is so rich with possibilities that it must be something we learn."

The words of Romulus were inspiring and prompted an idea. I asked Pesna to write Nivea's name in his language and that of the Greeks, which he knew. He wrote the symbols and showed how they matched the sounds, more or less. We said the name a little differently, so the symbols of Etruscan and Latin didn't work perfectly.

"Try this," suggested Remus. "If the sound is the same in all the languages, use a symbol like Greek or Etruscan, whichever is easiest. For the other sounds, make a new symbol."

Without knowing exactly what we were doing, we tried what Remus suggested. Pesna had no trouble with Nivea's name. He wrote most of it easily in both Greek and Etruscan, but not all of it. We wrote other names with the same result. All of us were surprised to find that our languages had different sounds in addition to different words.

Over the next few days, Romulus, Remus, and I worked with Pesna to come up with a set of symbols for our sounds. It was painstaking work that was both unpredictable and frustrating. Some of our words were almost identical, while others were so different that we had to create completely different symbols. At the end of our work, we had created a set of symbols that we thought matched the sounds of our language.

In the process of creating the symbols, I was able to write the names of everyone from our village. I also wrote some other words that had the sounds that were not in the names. I wrote the symbols, names, and words on a piece of parchment using a cut feather and a dark fluid made of wax and charcoal, as Pesna had suggested.

When I showed the symbols to Romulus, he understood the importance of what I had done. He had an idea with which all of us agreed.

"Make other copies of what Serena and Pesna have created," he suggested. "Each of us should keep a copy with our belongings. I know it will take a long time and will take us away from other chores. The effort will be worthwhile, however, so the symbols will not be lost. We will want others to know what has happened to us, and writing with symbols is the best way to do this."

It took days for us to make the copies. Everyone helped, including Pesna and some of the Martani. Creating the copies of the symbols took on a special meaning for us. Even though we were not yet telling our story, we all knew this was a first step. Once we all had copies of the symbols and practiced using them, we could write about our people and our journey. As odd as this sounds, the act of writing became so important to us that we all learned how to do it. Some were better than others, as was true of just about everything, but we all felt proud that we were able to tell about ourselves in a way that lived beyond us.

Chapter X

Feeling a mix of frustration and anger, Discordia sought a new ally. The Veiians were too far away and would not attack another Etruscan tribe. But there was an option.

"The Arroni will help us," she muttered to the Keres. "They are no match for the Tarquinians, but they can easily overcome this band of children. I will speak to them."

The leader of the Arroni was very taken by the beautiful stranger who had wandered into his village. She told Sergius of the group of young people who had recently joined the Martani, explaining how they had settled into a new village. She implied that the Martani were encouraging these people from the south to move into the area where the Arroni now lived.

The beautiful stranger said that the newcomers would be cutting down trees that day to build their shelters. She described the place they would be working, which angered Sergius even more. They would be in a forest that the Arroni claimed as their own.

The huts we had built were good enough for temporary use. They would not, however, give us enough protection to be warm when winter arrived. We decided to improve them by adding stronger posts and beams. After that, we would cover the walls with mud to keep out the wind.

"We have a favor to ask of you, Pesna," said Romulus. "We'd like to be excused from our work today so that we can cut some wood from the forest near the northern river. Our huts are fine now, but they will not be livable when winter arrives."

"You've been great workers," answered Pesna. "I would be a fool to deny your request. Would you like some of us to help you?"

"Thank you, but we can probably find all the wood we will need by ourselves. Besides, we'd feel guilty taking your people away from their duties. It's bad enough that we are taking time off during the harvest."

Gathering our tools and pulling a cart we had borrowed, we walked north along a narrow road. There were no forests near the village because all of the trees had been cut down for fuel, building materials, or to clear land for growing crops. The nearest *silva* was a little more than an hour's walk from the village. We had not been there before, but Pesna gave us directions and insisted that we would have no trouble finding the forest, which was true. It was in a valley on the east side of the road.

As soon as we arrived, Remus started marking trees to be cut. They had to be of a consistent size and thick enough to add strength to our huts. The rest of us got to work right away so we would finish as quickly as possible. We didn't know the area well, we were more than an hour from Martanum, and we had no weapons other than our cutting tools.

The assault by the Arroni was swift and effective. While we were focused on cutting trees, they must have surrounded us. All of a sudden, they were simply there, seeming to drift out of the forest like ghosts. There were more than forty of them on horses, and they were all fully armed.

"Come close together with our backs to one another," said Romulus. "Move slowly, and don't hold your cutting tools as weapons." His voice had an urgent tone, but it was not a shout. He hoped to avoid startling the attackers.

The leader of the warriors gave orders in a language I didn't understand. It was similar to our language, but the words made no sense to me. I doubt anyone else understood him, either. His men drew closer and brandished their weapons. None of them made an aggressive move, however.

Speaking in our language, the leader said, "I am Sergius, leader of the Arroni. You are our prisoners. If you do not resist us, you will not be harmed. We are going to take you from this place."

He gave his men orders, and the circle they had formed opened. They nudged their horses forward, showing that they wanted us to move in a specific direction, which we did. They did not hurry us along, just kept us moving at a steady pace.

Turning to me, Remus whispered, "Where is Nivea? She is always so attentive. Why did she not warn us?"

I looked around, embarrassed that I had not been concerned about Nivea. He was right. She was nowhere to be seen, which was so unlike her.

"Don't look up at once, but I see her near the top of the hill ahead of us. The Arroni either didn't see Nivea, or they paid no attention to her," said Romulus. He waited for a moment, glanced up, and said, "Nivea seems to know where we are going. She has stayed in front of us and is dodging from tree to tree to remain hidden. The Arroni are so focused on us that they are not looking in her direction at all."

Our captors were unaggressive. They did not threaten us and gave us several rest breaks. We were able to eat and drink as we walked. After a time, Sergius gave us a warning.

"Do not think we are weak. We need you healthy. With you as our slaves, we will be able to mine more iron than ever before. You are young, so we will get many years of work out of you."

By late that afternoon, we reached some rocky hills. Guards were stationed around the base of one of the hills. Near its top was the opening of a cave. The Arroni drove us up the hill toward the cave, which we entered cautiously.

"You will have company in the cave," mumbled Sergius. "Our other slaves have been there for a long time."

The interior of the cave was dimly lit by torches and cooking fire. It took a moment for our eyes to adjust to the poor light. What we saw stunned us. The slaves were centaurs, half horse and half human.

"Don't be afraid. We're captives just like you. Through Nivea, we knew you were coming. I am Silvano."

Nivea, who was standing beside Silvano, pranced over to us. Her being there was comforting yet confusing. How did she know where the cave was? How did she get past the guards? How did Silvano learn from Nivea that we were coming?

"You have many questions, I am sure," added Silvano. "Come and join us. There isn't much food, but we will share what we have."

"Thank you," said Romulus meekly. "I think I can speak for all of us. We are honored to be in your presence and by your generosity, but we have no idea what to say to you. All of us grew up with stories of the magical centaurs, but we thought your existence was a legend."

"Well, we're not a legend," said Equinius, one of the other centaurs, with a laugh, "and we can't be too magical, can we, or we wouldn't be here."

As they ate, Silvano explained how they arrived in this place and these circumstances. "We came here from Greece after a conflict with Peirithous, king of the Lapiths. We were driven away, and our journey took us to many places. On the way, we crossed into the land of the Gorgons and were cursed. These dreadful creatures condemned us to serve the next humans we met until other humans set us free. When we reached Etruria, we met the Arroni, and we were enslaved, in accordance with the curse of the Gorgons."

"What kept you from turning to stone when you saw them?" asked Anna.

"We had the good sense not to look at them," said Equinius. "At least we got that right."

"Why don't you run away?" asked Remus.

"The curse of the Gorgon sisters is too strong," replied Silvano. "When we first encountered the Arroni, we scoffed at them. We knew from the way they sat on their horses that they were not good riders. It would be fairly easy to escape. But when we attempted to flee, we could not. Our legs barely moved, and exhaustion overcame us. The same has happened every time we tried to leave."

"Are the Arroni aware of the curse?" asked Romulus.

"They seem not to be," answered Silvano. "They were surprised when they happened upon us, and even more so when they found we could not resist them. We didn't have the strength to lift our weapons. The curse is very strong.

Equinius sighed and said, "What's worse is that the idiotic Arroni think they are superhumans because they were able to overcome us."

Nico, who was standing beside Nivea, stepped forward. Sheepishly, he said something that caused both the humans and centaurs to break into raucous laughter. Even Nivea joined in with a series of barks to show she understood what the boy had said.

"May I sit on you, Silvano? I have never been on a horse or a centaur."

When he stopped laughing, Silvano waved the boy over. Motioning to his side, he grasped the boy's hand and helped him onto his back. From the look on his face, we could see that Nico was enthralled. What he said next changed everything.

"Why can't we just ride away with you?" Nico suggested. "You said the curse would be broken if humans set you free. We are humans. We can set you free."

"But the Arroni have horses and weapons. We have nothing to protect you or ourselves. We would be slaughtered," argued Gaius, the oldest of the Albans.

"You are right about that," said Silvano, "but we know the Arroni. They are not good riders, and they are probably not very good fighters. If the spell is broken, we can easily outrun their horses."

"How will we know if the spell is broken?" asked Gaius. "If it isn't we will have no chance against them."

"Let me test the strength of the spell with Silvano," said Nico. "I will ride him, and we will start to run away. If we succeed, the rest of you can come after us. If Silvano is hindered by the spell, we can claim that we were just playing. I'm a small boy. The Arroni could not possibly believe that I could force a centaur to take a chance with his life for me."

"The boy's idea is worth considering," said Silvano, "but it does involve risks to all of us. Let's take some time to talk about it. And I commend you, Nico, both for your idea and for your ability to sit properly on a centaur with no prior experience. You are a born rider."

Over the next few days, all of us did as the Arroni commanded. We worked the iron mines diligently, creating the impression that we had resigned ourselves to our fate. At night, we worked out the details of the plan. Through it all, Nivea managed to stay out of sight of our captors.

On the fourth day, we began our trek from the cave to the mines as we usually did. Along the way, the trail skirted the edge of a forest. It was there that we executed the plan. The centaurs believed that they would be at a great advantage running through the trees because of the poor horsemanship of the Arroni.

As he had suggested, Nico jumped onto Silvano's back, a move the two of them and the rest of us had practiced over the past several days. Silvano stood still for a moment and then started running. Startled, the Arroni did nothing but watch him. Seeing that he was not hampered by the curse, we each mounted the centaur with whom we had practiced and took off. Nivea ran effortlessly beside us.

The Arroni attempted to give chase, but as Silvano had said, their riding skills left much to be desired. They had difficulty making their way through the forest because they had to steer the horses while remaining balanced, causing a delay at each turn. We simply held onto the centaurs, who moved effortlessly through the trees. The sensation of being carried by the centaurs was incredible, almost like flying.

Reaching the open area at the edge of the forest, the centaurs moved even faster. When I looked behind us, none of the Arroni were in sight. We continued on for several hours, and still no Arroni were to be seen.

Silvano led us up a small hill and stopped. From this vantage point, we could see that no one was trailing us. We dismounted and thanked the centaurs who had carried us to freedom. All of us scanned the area around the hill and still saw no signs of the Arroni.

"This is the land of the Tarquinians. They are not allied with the Arroni, and I think you will be welcomed here. The city of Tarquinii is not far away toward the south. The people have been successful with agriculture, mining metals, and trade."

Romulus clasped Silvano's arm and said, "Thanks to you and your people, Silvano, we are safe."

"It is we who should be thankful, Romulus. You have set us free. May your future be glorious. We will never forget you."

"What will you do now?" asked Remus.

"We would like to return to Olympus, our true home," said Silvano. "I have no idea how we can do that because we don't know where the gateway is. No matter how long it takes, we will find it."

Nivea walked a short distance away and sat at the edge of a cliff. Behind her, clouds began to gather. A slight opening appeared in their center, and in the distance, a mountain could be seen. The centaurs were illuminated with a magical light that came from the mountain in the clouds.

"It's the gateway," said Equinius joyfully, and he reared onto his back legs.

Silvano paced to Nivea's side, bowed, and touched her head. Taking a deep breath, he leaped off the cliff into the clouds. He was followed by the other centaurs who, to our wonderment, soared toward the mountain. In a moment, the clouds dissipated, the centaurs were gone, and everything was as it had been before.

Chapter XI

"You have been thwarted at every turn, Discordia. Why don't you just let the humans decide their own fate?" suggested the goddess Ceres. She watched the humans helplessly from Olympus.

"That is not my way," grumbled Discordia. "As much as I have enjoyed seeing them suffer, it is not enough."

"I must admit that I regret what I did for you," said Vulcanus. "This group of humans has earned my admiration."

For a time, we stood there looking at where the centaurs had disappeared. None of us knew what to think about this astonishing turn of events.

Katia, my friend since childhood, interrupted our thoughts with a difficult question. "What will happen now? We are not much better off than when we started. In fact, things are probably worse because we don't know where we are."

"Silvano said that Tarquinii is not far away, and that we might be welcome there," answered Remus. "We should probably try to find the people of Tarquinii and hope for the best."

Nico pointed toward the south and said, "There seems to be a village in that direction. Silvano said Tarquinii was that way."

"You are clever to remember what he said and notice the buildings," I said. "We are lucky to have you."

The boy blushed at my words, but I know he was grateful for my comment. I was the oldest girl in our group, and he was the youngest of all of us. I had cared for him as a child, and in our situation, he probably thought of me as a substitute for his mother. I am sure he missed her and the rest of his family as well.

"We have no choice other than to go over and see how we are received," suggested Romulus.

And so we walked toward the structures, being alert for anyone who might approach us. Even though we hoped that Silvano was right, we had learned a difficult lesson from the Arroni.

Nothing prepared us for what took place when we reached the structures. There was not a single person or animal to be seen. The structures stood alone with no places for fires or storage, and there were no signs of human activity.

The sounds of riders caused all of us to turn

at once. We huddled together defensively as some horsemen drew near. They were armed, but their casual manner suggested that they were not aggressive. Their leader spoke to us, but his words had no meaning to me.

Romulus answered in our language, "We are travelers who mean you no harm."

"You speak the language of the people of Alba Longa. We heard of your arrival from the Martani, and that you disappeared. I am called Thefarie," said a man who appeared to be their leader.

"We were taken against our will by the Arroni," said Romulus. "We escaped with the centaurs."

"And where are the centaurs? We know the legend, but we have never seen any."

"The centaurs are more than a legend," said Remus. "We rode them to freedom. They carried us to that hill, and there we parted ways. They flew off into the clouds and said they would return to Olympus."

The Tarquinians smiled at one another and said something we did not understand. It was easy to tell, however, that they didn't believe us. Given how strange the story sounded, none of us tried to persuade them of the truth.

Katia asked the question all of us were thinking. "Where are all the people? Your houses are beautiful, but no one is around."

"This is not where we live. This is our necropolis, the place for our dead."

"Why do you create such lavish homes for the dead?" asked Nico impulsively.

Although Nico's question seemed inappropriate to us, Thefarie was not upset at all. He seemed to relish the opportunity to answer.

"Long ago, we cremated our dead in sacred fires. Then we learned a different way from the people across the sea. They changed our thinking. Now we believe that death is not an end for us. It is the beginning of the journey to the afterlife. We treat our dead well so they make the journey quickly and do not linger here. Their comfort after death will help them move on. We all look forward to what comes next."

"You speak our language well," said Remus. "We learned a little of your language from the Martani. How did you learn our language?"

"My grandmother came from the south, and she was one of my caretakers. I first learned your tongue from her. The Tarquinians have traded with the people to the south for many years. For as long as I can remember, I traveled with my father to the Tiber River and beyond. Most of us can speak several languages, so we can trade successfully."

Thefarie turned to a structure that was being built. "This will be my tomb. My wife will share it with me. But enough about my tomb. Why are you here in our land?"

"Silvano, the leader of the centaurs, said that your people might need workers. We have experience herding and farming. From the Martani, we learned a little metal working," answered Romulus.

Thefarie answered in a puzzling way, at least to my understanding. "We could use help, but we cannot offer you work. The Martani told us the story of the Veiians and your sundering. Veii is part of our alliance. You cannot stay here, or they might consider it an affront."

Hearing Thefarie's words was a disappointment to all of us. We could think of nothing to say. For myself, I felt a degree of hopelessness I had never sensed before.

To his credit, Thefarie saw our dismay. "We can offer you food and water. If you want, you may spend the night here in the necropolis. Do not be afraid. The spirits of our dead have passed on to the next life because we have honored them so. My people sometimes spend the night here to celebrate special occasions."

At his direction, several of Thefarie's men rode back to Tarquinii to obtain supplies for us. Thefarie and his other men stayed with us. They took us to shelters where we could spend the night. The shelters were used by the workers who built the tombs. They stayed in them when storms struck or if it was necessary to spend the night.

While we waited, we shared the story of how we came here. The Tarquinians were intrigued by what we had gone through. We, in turn, were equally fascinated to hear about the necropolis, whose tombs were far more elaborate than the homes in which we lived.

Thefarie guided us around the necropolis, which consisted of dozens of stone buildings. In those that were open, we could see that some had several rooms, and many of the walls in each tomb were painted beautifully.

"Your homes must be elegant if these are your tombs," said Katia. She, like the rest of us, was awestruck by the buildings.

"Our homes are less elegant than our tombs," responded Thefarie. "We came to believe that the afterlife was more important than our life in this world. Our time here is short. The afterlife is forever. We are willing to live modestly now in order to enjoy a better life in the next world."

"Do all of your people have such elaborate tombs?" asked Romulus.

"Those who are successful always have tombs. They start the construction when they are alive to oversee the process. Poorer people, of course, don't have tombs. They are cremated, and their ashes are kept in urns."

As Thefarie guided us through the necropolis, he pointed to some tombs that were carved into a hillside. "Many years ago, we cut our tombs into the soft rocks of these hills. As we became better builders, we made our tombs freestanding. The Greek traders taught us some of their techniques. In my tomb, the wall paintings will be stories from the Greek war with Troy."

Most of the tombs were square or rectangle shaped. One, however, was round, and even had a domed roof. Nico, always curious, asked, "Why is this tomb different from the others? Is there a reason why it is not finished?"

"That is a new style of tomb," explained Thefarie. "Many of our huts are round, but we did not know how to make the domed roof. Traders from across the sea and tribes from the north showed us how to create the round roof. We were not successful, as you can see, but we are hopeful. The owner of this tomb is my cousin. She and her husband are going to Ichnusa, an island in the great sea, to look for workers to complete their tomb. We have heard that the people of Ichnusa have a special talent for building domes."

The time passed quickly, and Thefarie was gracious in answering our questions. His men returned with several horses laden with food and water. There were supplies for several days as well as food for the evening meal.

Before he left us, Thefarie said something that was both pleasing and unsettling. "You seem like fine people, and I wish I could welcome you into our tribe. I know my grandmother and the others from the south would enjoy you. Our ties with the Veiians are such that I cannot do this.

"Moreover, the story of your journey shows that you are somehow engaged with the gods, some of whom seem to test you at every turn, while others protect you. Your journey reminds me of the story of Odysseus, who after years of wandering, returned home to reclaim his kingdom."

Looking at Nivea, he continued. "Even your dog seems to be special. From what you have told me, she has lived many years, yet she looks as spry as a puppy. She listens as if she understands every word, and when we approached the first time, she showed no protectiveness, sensing that we meant you no harm.

"We urge you to move on and to leave the lands of the Etruscan people. I can assure your safety in the lands of Tarquinii, but not beyond. Be wary of everyone. Thus far, you have been fortunate, but the Fates have been known to change."

With that, Thefarie and his men left. We were left alone in the necropolis, which without their presence, became a more eerie place.

Nivea's slight bark changed the mood. She turned and walked toward the shelter that Thefarie had indicated. We gathered up the food and water and followed her. The simple act of walking from the necropolis to the workers' shelter changed our mood. We went from a feeling of uncertainty to appreciation that we had a place to spend the night.

"Thefarie urged us to leave the lands of the Etruscans," said Remus. "Does anyone have any idea how extensive their lands are or even the directions in which they are located?"

None of us did, but Katia had a suggestion that helped. "All of us know something about the Etruscans and the other people in our land. Together we can figure out which way we should go to avoid the Etruscans."

"They are mostly north of our home," said Nico, "and mostly along the coast of the great sea."

"The mountains separate the Etruscans from the tribes of the east," added Gaius. "The Umbrians live across the mountains. They are allied with the people of Alba Longa. Maybe we should head east."

"But what about the Veiians?" asked Anna.

"They are south of us, so they should not be a problem. But the Falisci support the Veiians. It's best that we avoid them," suggested Remus.

The conversation went on until we came to a consensus. We agreed that we should head north and east, a journey that would take us across the mountains and out of the Etruscan territory. The journey would not be easy, as the central mountains were rugged. They stretched far to the north and south past our village. Nonetheless, we had no choice. The Etruscans surrounded us, and the sea was to the west.

As we had done before, we huddled together in the shelter. Two of us at a time took turns serving as guards, joined by Nivea. The night passed without incident, and in the morning, we were in a better mood than the day before.

The rising sun showed us the direction in which we should travel. A mountain in the distance would help us maintain our path through the day. With enough food and water for several days, and no obvious threats, we expected to make good time. We set off with Nivea leading us on a well-used trail that wound through the rolling hills.

Chapter XII

Discordia was no longer as upset with the small band of humans. She was beginning to enjoy tormenting them, much as she had the Greeks and Trojans as they engaged in war for more than ten years.

The Keres, however, were not as pleased. They needed death in order to be gratified, and the misery of the Albans satisfied them not at all.

Knowing the Keres well, Discordia soothed them. "There will soon be souls on which you can feed. I have told the Vulci where they can find the perfect victim for a sacrifice, and made them believe that the sacrifice will bring them more riches."

For two days, we walked toward the mountain in the distance. We did not travel very quickly because we encountered no one and did not feel threatened. In addition to the food we carried, we were able to pick fruit and hunt small animals. There were larger animals like aurochs, deer, and boar, but our weapons were not suitable for hunting them. At night, we made crude shelters with sticks and brush.

"This reminds me of our home," sighed Katia, as we descended from the crest of a hill around noon on the second day. "The meadows would be ideal for grazing animals, and the forests would provide us with wood for our homes. The ground is so fertile that our crops would hardly need tending."

Most of us agreed with her, but we knew that what she suggested was unlikely. As Remus pointed out, we had no seeds, no livestock, and nothing to trade. We had to keep moving until we found a friendly tribe who would give us an opportunity to work.

It was the growling of Nivea that told us we were not alone. When we reached the valley at the base of the hill, dozens of armed men were waiting for us. They did not seem threatening, and their leader spoke to us in our language.

"I am Vibenna, the leader of Vulci. You are in our land."

"Thefarie gave us safe passage," answered Romulus. His tone was respectful, as he did not want to offend Vibenna.

"So I have heard," answered Vibenna, "but Thefarie has no standing here. This is the territory of Vulci." The leader's voice changed to a somewhat friendlier tone. "You are welcome here. Thefarie said you were from the region of Alba Longa. Is this true?"

"Yes, our settlement is near Alba Longa," answered Romulus. "Do you know the area?"

With an odd look on his face, Vibenna said, "Yes, we know the legends of the founding of Alba Longa by Aeneas. We would like to hear your stories sometime. But that will come later. Thefarie told us you were eager to work. We will give you as much work as you can handle. We mine metal in the mountains and trade with the Greeks. We need good workers."

Turning to his men, he spoke in his own language, and they started walking. Pointing toward the north, Vibenna said, "Come with us."

Given the number of armed men, we had no choice but to follow Vibenna. Through the whole exchange, no one other than Vibenna spoke. His warriors barely acknowledged us. It was a very unsettling feeling. Even so, Vibenna seemed to be offering us the opportunity to work and perhaps settle in a place that reminded us of our home.

Nivea stayed between Romulus and Remus. She was not aggressive toward the strangers, but she remained cautious and growled softly. Like the rest of us, she seemed to recognize that we were powerless.

After about an hour, Romulus asked Vibenna, "How far will we be walking?"

"It is not much farther," he answered, but said

nothing more.

Soon we spotted some buildings in the distance. No people were around, and because of our experience with the Tarquinians, we knew that the place we saw was a necropolis. There were tombs of every kind as well as carved stones that seemed to mark graves.

We passed by the necropolis and approached the city of Vulci, which was built on a hill. Well-dressed people walked among the buildings, and workers went about their business. The buildings were elegant, at least to our eyes, and the people seemed prosperous.

The workers in the city did many of the things we were familiar with, like bringing food to market, making clothing, and selling goods. Among them were some people doing curious things. Some were working stone to make statues. We had never seen people carve stone, only wood. We slowed down as we walked by because what they were doing seemed to us to be impossible.

Throughout the city were groups of people working metal. Furnaces that burned wood and coal were used to melt red-colored stones mixed with charcoal to produce iron. From the iron, other workers made tools and weapons. We had never seen so much iron, which was very costly to obtain through trade.

Another group was making pottery bowls and containers. This was something that was done in most villages, and some of us had learned this skill. What was unusual was the color of the pottery. Unlike the red or brown pottery that we made, the pottery of Vulci was shiny and black. At one point, we were very close to some finished pots, and I reached out to touch one. A nearby worker shouted something I did not understand, and I quickly pulled my hand away, but not before feeling how smooth it was.

Our presence did not seem to bother the people of Vulci. Like Vibenna, they seemed to be waiting for us. We were not sure how to interpret this, but we hoped for the best.

Some of the young people in the town stopped their work for a moment as we walked by. They stared at us, but like the adults, they said nothing. Katia nudged me and pointed to a handsome boy, but after making a faint smile, he quickly turned away.

Vibenna led us to an open space near the center of town. He dismissed his warriors and suggested that we rest in the shade of some buildings. After showing us where we could get water from a spring, he said he would soon be back and walked off.

"This is really weird," said Romulus. "Here we are in an unfamiliar land, yet no one is surprised. The leader of the people leaves us alone in their city with no guards around. It makes no sense."

"Given the terrible things that have happened to us recently, we should probably be grateful that everyone is so complacent," answered Remus. "Even so, I'm not comfortable with our situation. We have no real weapons, and we have almost no idea where we are."

"That is probably why no one seems concerned or very interested," suggested Nico. "There is not much threat from a group of young people who are lost, dirty, and have no weapons."

We all laughed at what Nico said because he was right. We were hardly a threat to these people, and we had almost no idea where we were.

Vibenna soon returned with several companions. He made no introductions, other than to say that the people with him would show us our living quarters and help us find work in a few days. They led us to a cluster of shelters on the outskirts of the city. The huts were basic structures with thatched roofs made of straw and mud-plastered walls. One of the people spoke briefly to us. She said that food would be brought to us, and that tomorrow we would start our work. She also said there might be danger nearby and warned us not to go far from the shelters. She pointed to a nearby spring and said the water was drinkable, and showed us.

"Maybe the gods are finally on our side," suggested Gaius. "Since we have no choice in the matter, let's just relax."

At that moment, a few people came to the shelter carrying food for us. They put the food on a long table nearby, bowed their heads to us, and walked away. The way they behaved seemed almost as if they were servants and we were their masters.

We ate well, and though some of the food was known to us, some was not. The unfamiliar food was flavored with spices we did not know. Our people used no spices other than what we could grow. Salt was added to some foods to preserve them and for flavor. Occasionally, Greek traders would share some of their food with us, and it had some of the same spices as the food the Vulci provided for us.

Time passed quickly as we ate and talked. The sun set, and as night fell, we decided not to build a fire. There was no wood nearby, we were tired, and given the events of the day, sleeping seemed to be a wise choice. As we usually did, several of us shared watch duties with Nivea. We were certain that the Vulci had their own guards around their city, with a few extra near us, so we felt safe.

I was in a deep sleep when a hand touched my shoulder and I heard my name. When I woke, I thought I was dreaming. Romulus and Remus were sitting on the ground beside me, as was Milo. I rubbed my eyes to be sure I wasn't dreaming and started to talk. Milo signaled me to be quiet, and the worried look on his face told me that something was wrong.

The four of us woke the others silently, and

we gathered in one of the huts. The waxing moon cast just a little light, so it was difficult to see one another. Milo spoke softly, and it was also hard to hear him. His words were chilling.

"I will be brief, but you are all at risk here. The Vulci are holding Chiara captive. She will be sacrificed at some point in the next few days. They also plan to sacrifice each of you over time."

"How was Chiara captured, and why would they consider sacrificing her or us?" asked Remus.

"Before we reached the ship, we were attacked by a band of Arroni. In the battle several of our men were killed and Chiara was captured. We were taken by surprise, because we thought they were a band of traders. They must have known who we were, especially Chiara. They came to us on horses with a wagon of pottery jars and cloth. The Arroni invited Chiara to look at the goods. When she reached the wagon, one of them grabbed her, dragged her into the wagon, and drove off. The others attacked immediately. Once the wagon was well away from us, they broke off and fled. There was no doubt that they came specifically for her.

"After the attack, I went back to the Martani to see if they could help us. They explained what might have happened. Small groups of Etruscans, including some people of Vulci, are beginning to consider the Greeks, my people, to be threatening. We have traded with them for many years, and I thought they were good partners.

These people seem to be consumed by greed, and no amount of wealth can satisfy them. They have begun to worship Aeneas because he was an enemy of Greece at Troy before he joined the gods on Olympus. Pesna said that the Arroni might sell Chiara to the Vulci, who would then sacrifice her."

"But Aeneas has never asked for sacrifice," I insisted, offended that one of the heroes of our people would be so disparaged. "Aeneas is an important part of our founding stories and brought to our people the notion of *pietas*, being dutiful to family, friends, and tribe. How can this be?"

At that moment, I was swept away by emotions, and I am not sure which was more troubling. I was concerned about Chiara, of course, as well as our own safety. But just as worrisome was the idea that reverence for Aeneas, who might have been our ancestor, would be distorted to the point of human sacrifice.

"But how did you end up here?" asked Remus. "Aren't you in jeopardy, too?"

"I joined a group of traders and came here as soon as I could. I acted as if I had heard nothing about the attack. Chiara knows I am here, but the Vulci suspect nothing. I learned about you from Vibenna."

"What can we do?" asked Romulus. "There are only a few of us, and we haven't many weapons. There must be some way to free Chiara and escape."

"Vibenna says the sacrifice will take place in the coming days. We have a little time to plan and prepare," answered Milo. "The Vulci want you to work for them, so pretend you know nothing. I will come back tomorrow night. Do not show that you know me, and I will do the same if Vibenna mentions you."

As Milo turned to go, Remus grabbed his arm and said, "You are a good friend for gambling with your own life to help Chiara and us. We owe you."

Chapter XIII

Aeneas glared at Discordia. She had caused the Vulci to worship him in a dishonorable way and endangered his descendants. As a former mortal, however, he could not directly interfere in the whims of a god like Discordia.

He was not alone in his displeasure. Some of the other gods felt that Discordia's actions were petty. The Albans had been faithful to the gods and showed great strength of character. But for now, they would simply observe to see what happened. The destiny of the Albans was in their own hands.

The next day was even more confusing. A group of young people and adults brought us food in the morning. They ate with us and attempted conversation. Some of them knew a few words in our language, but we knew none of theirs. Their few words and our gestures and expressions let us communicate enough so we felt comfortable with them.

Their kindness toward us was offset by what seemed to be apprehension. They shared worried looks with one another and often looked outside the shelter as if they expected someone to arrive. After a time, Vibenna returned and the others left. He led us through the city and pointed out their temples, the buildings where the leaders met, his home, and other sights. We walked beyond the city itself to an agricultural area used for growing crops and grazing animals. None of us had ever seen so many cattle and sheep in one place or such large fields of wheat and beans.

As we reached the far end of a field, Vibenna said, "We are very proud of our fields and farms. Because you have experience with agriculture, we would like you to work here during the harvest season. Once the crops have been brought in, we will teach you some of our other industries. Our iron mines are in those hills, and we could use your help. Traders from other places across the sea value our iron tools and weapons. Our pottery, especially that which is black, is prized as well. You will be apprenticed to skilled workers so you will learn our trades."

"May we start working at once?" asked Romulus.

The question that Romulus asked was curious at first, but we quickly agreed with him. Doing something that was normal to us would be satisfying, and our effort would show Vibenna and the other Vulci that we were sincere in our search for a new home.

Vibenna waved to one of the farmers, and he walked over. The two of them spoke in the Etruscan language, and the farmer smiled at us. He led us into the field where some other young people were working. The task of reaping grain was familiar to all of us, and we set to work at once. It was a relief to have something customary to do.

And so we spent the day, working in the fields, enjoying the company of others who were our own age. Nivea wandered among us and was far friendlier to the young people and the farmers than she had been to Vibenna and his guards. In this nurturing environment, it was not long before we learned a little of the language of the Etruscans, and they of ours. By the end of the day, we had made new friends and earned the gratitude of the farmers for whom we worked. They gave us a few small pieces of metal, which we didn't understand, and baskets of different foods that we could take back to our shelters. For this moment, at least, our lives were settled.

Milo returned late that night, waking us as he did before. The news he carried was not good. Vibenna said that the sacrifice would take place the next night when the full moon reached its highest point in the sky. He told us the plan he wanted to execute. Because the Vulci trusted him,

Milo would try to get close to Chiara tomorrow. Then he would free her, and the two of them would slip away unnoticed. She was not heavily guarded because Vibenna had no reason to suspect a rescue.

"That is a courageous plan," suggested Remus, "but it puts both of you in a difficult situation. I can't imagine that you would be able to escape successfully."

"If I don't do something, Chiara will die. The worst outcome for my plan is that I die with her. If we manage to get away, we can recruit help and come back to rescue all of you."

"Isn't there something that we can do to help?" I asked.

"You are already in danger, but I think it is not immediate," insisted Milo. "I saw you working in the fields today, and you seemed happy. Later, the farmers told Vibenna that you were good workers. He sees you as a source of dependable labor, and the farmers are in need of your help picking crops while they are in season."

As much as we wanted to help, we recognized that there was nothing we could do, and no one had a better plan. Milo promised that if he could think of a way for us to help, he would let us know.

None of us slept well that night, and our work the next day did little to distract us. What was even more troubling was that both the farmers and the other workers behaved differently toward us, as if they knew something was going to happen.

Throughout the day, we were alert for any signs that would suggest that Milo's plan for Chiara had succeeded or failed. The fields where we worked were just outside the walls of the city, and if there had been a conflict of any kind, we would have heard it. Without knowing otherwise, we were hopeful that his plan had succeeded.

At the end of the day, Vibenna came to the field alone. He seemed pleased and invited us to an event in the city. We walked with him to a central square where hundreds of people had gathered. A few of them were armed soldiers, but the majority were not. Among the crowd were the young people we had worked with, their families, and the farmers. They mingled among us as we shared the food that had been provided. Time passed quickly, and with the evening darkness surrounding us, torches were lit around the square.

Because we were not sure what was going on, we clustered together and stayed at the edge of the square. It was not surprising when Vibenna ascended some steps and prepared to address the crowd. He seemed to enjoy his leadership role and the importance that came with it.

Although we could not understand what Vibenna said, his speech was filled with broad gestures and solemn words. None of the leaders in our village ever spoke this way, but we heard that such things happened in other cities.

And then time seemed to stop. From a doorway behind Vibenna walked Chiara and Milo with their hands tied and guards at their side. She looked at us but showed no sign of recognition, and Milo never raised his eyes. We had no idea what to do. There were few of us, and we had no weapons.

Chiara and Milo were marched down the steps and to a wall at the far end of the square. They were forced to kneel down, and their hands were tied to iron rings in the ground. This was to be the place of sacrifice, and Vibenna would be the executioner. An aide marched ceremoniously from a building and handed him an ornate silver knife that he would use to end their lives. All seemed hopeless.

The events that occurred next are seared in my memory. Several people in the crowd started shouting, and most of the others joined them. Although I did not understand their words, to me, it seemed as if they were objecting to the sacrifice. A few people at the front of the crowd ran to Vibenna's side, as did some of the armed men. Dozens of people moved in front of Chiara and Milo to protect them, and in the melee, Vibenna's aide dropped the knife and fled.

"Come, Nivea," shouted Romulus, and the two of them worked their way through the crowd until they reached Chiara and Milo.

Seeing the knife on the ground, Romulus

picked it up and cut the ropes that bound them. "Stay close to Nivea," he whispered to them, "and don't worry about me."

Nivea led them to us, while Romulus protected them from the rear. Some of the Vulci surrounded us, making it hard for Vibenna and his guards to reach us. The armed warriors at Vibenna's side started to move against the crowd, but other warriors opposed them. Some in the crowd around us pulled small weapons from their tunics, and those who were unarmed picked up stones from the edge of the square.

As chaotic as the scene was, it became more so in a moment. Nivea growled loudly, and as she did, the wind rose and blew out the torches. Clouds formed out of nowhere, and lightning flashed. The wooden buildings near the square and in other parts of the city were damaged by the wind, and debris flew all around us. People from other parts of the city flooded into the square.

Most frightening of all was the appearance of a shadowy figure that set upon Vibenna's warriors, causing them to panic. This wraith moved among them, impervious to their swords, but did nothing to harm either them or any of those nearby.

Several of the young Vulci led us out of the mass of people and pointed to a road leading through the city wall. Milo, who knew the area well, ran in front with Nivea at his side. Our friends from Vulci stayed behind to prevent anyone from threatening us. Despite our panic, Romulus stopped, turned, and shouted *gratia amici*. Even if they did not know our language, they understood that he was thanking them as friends.

The light of the full moon allowed Milo to lead us safely out of the city. Whenever I looked back, however, I could see that a fog had formed behind us. Pursuers would not be able to see us. There was a river nearby that could have been the source of the fog, but it seemed almost supernatural as it wound its way along the road.

We stayed on the main road until it split. Milo took us on the left fork, which was less traveled. We continued on for several hours. Because no one came after us and we encountered no one ahead of us, we made good time.

At one point, the road made a sharp turn to the north. Rather than staying on the road, Milo headed down a small trail that led toward the east. The trail quickly became more difficult and rose steeply. He explained that if the Vulci followed on foot, they would be far behind us, and if they came on horseback, the animals could not climb the hill. He promised that we would be on a better trail in an hour or so.

In the moonlight we could see that the trail we were on was almost vertical, and that the hill was in reality a cliff. We struggled in several places, especially near the top, but understood that the steepness would protect us. It was a relief to reach the grassy area at the top.

By this time, we were all exhausted, and Romulus thought it was best if we stopped and rested. It was only then that we realized that we had barely spoken to one another for the past few hours. I ran to Chiara and we hugged one another, tearful with joy. The others did the same, and we could not thank Milo enough for what he had done for Chiara and us. As eager as we were to hear the story of what happened, we would have to wait, because the most important thing all of us needed was sleep. No one was capable of serving as a guard, so we just huddled together and slept on the ground, praying that Nivea would warn us if anyone approached.

The rising sun startled all of us into wakefulness. It was above the nearby trees, and we were almost in a panic, having slept so late. After a moment of gathering our thoughts, we began to talk with one another about our situation.

"We have no food, no water, and no weapons other than the agricultural tools we carried away from the fields," sighed Romulus, "but we are unhurt, as are Chiara and Milo."

"And we have Milo to guide us," added Nico with a smile. He then turned to Milo and asked, "You will be able to guide us, won't you?"

"I know where we are, and I am familiar with the area," answered Milo. "What is more crucial now, however, is finding food and water."

"From this high point, we should be able to spot a nearby stream," said Remus. "There are some fruit and nut trees nearby, so we will at least have a little food."

Nivea's barking caught our attention, and we were alarmed at once. Because we were at the top of the cliff on a flat area, there was no place to hide. All we could think to do was run down the hill away from the path that had brought us here.

Chapter XIV

The Keres had been gratified with the violence that had taken place in Vulci. There had been only a few deaths, but that small number of souls had satisfied them.

Discordia, however, was completely beside herself. There had been no sacrifice, and although some of the Vulci had become entranced with greed, most had not. It was this larger group that now controlled the city. She would have to find other ways to carry out her wishes and torment the Albans further.

After just a short distance, Romulus held up his hand as a signal to stop. "Nivea's barking doesn't have a sense of urgency," he said in a low voice. "Stay together here, and I'll go to her."

Romulus ran in the direction from which the barking came and disappeared down the hill into a cluster of trees. In a moment, he reappeared and waved at us, signaling that we should come over. What we found was better than we could have imagined. Not far away was a small stream. We would have water, and with a little luck, there would be fish or frogs in the stream. Berry bushes grew nearby, as did some fruit trees.

Although we were all thirsty and hungry, Milo urged caution. Others undoubtedly knew about the stream, and there was no reason to expect them to be friendly. Romulus, Remus, and Milo went first and scouted the area. Seeing no signs of people, they waved us down.

After drinking from the stream, we promptly went for the berries and fruit. We pulled them from where they grew and ate them on the spot. Once we had something in our bellies, we looked for fish and frogs. Although there were no frogs, fish were living in the stream. We made small baskets of the kind that we had played with as little children, and with them, we caught enough fish for a decent meal. Thankfully, several of us had pieces of flint, so we were able to start a fire and cook the fish.

"So tell us, Milo" said Remus, "how were you discovered?"

Shaking his head, Milo answered, "It was a case of bad luck. One of the traders told Vibenna that I had traded with the Albans before and might know Chiara. That was enough for him, and he sent his men after me. He never questioned me to see if what was said about me was true. He had me imprisoned, and the first that Chiara knew about my plight was when she was led from the hut for the sacrifice and saw that I had been found out. Things happened so quickly that I resigned myself to my fate. When I saw the people of Vulci rebel against the sacrifice, I was shocked. Vibenna had become a powerful leader, but he was obsessed by the need to acquire riches. Most of the Vulci, however, seemed disturbed at how he and a few others were trying to change their customs. Their willingness to stand up to him is a tribute to their honor and bravery."

Chiara, who was normally very talkative, had barely spoken since her rescue. I turned to her and asked, "What was it like?"

Surprisingly, she smiled and answered, "The whole thing, from the kidnapping to this moment, has been like a bad dream. I kept hoping to wake up and it would all be over. What I found strange was that the Arroni and the Vulci treated me so well, other than imprisoning me."

"How can you say that?" asked Katia. "You were kidnapped, imprisoned, and threatened with death. I would have been beside myself."

"I know it's hard to believe, but from the little I understood of their conversation, they valued me as a sacrifice because I was an Alban. They fed me well, treated me with respect, and gave me fine clothes. It has something to do with their worship of Aeneas."

"But Aeneas has never asked for human sacrifice," I blurted out.

"That is true, Serena" agreed Chiara, "but Vibenna and some of the wealthier of the Vulci were convinced that the sacrifice of someone from Alba Longa would make them even richer. They claim that Aeneas is their ancestor, and that our founding story is wrong."

"Which story?" asked Nico.

Romulus answered carefully, not wishing to misspeak and offend the gods. We had heard the old stories since we were small children, and our village held them and the gods in great respect.

"This story took place hundreds of years ago after the war between the Greeks and Trojans. Aeneas, who was an ally of the Trojans and fought with them, fled with his family and others from Troy by ship. He was one of the bravest of the Trojan warriors, and the gods promised that he would not die in Troy.

"After many difficult adventures, they arrived on the shores of our land. King Latinus welcomed the Trojans, and Aeneas soon fell in love with Lavinia, the daughter of Latinus. A rival for Lavinia, Turnus, became jealous of Aeneas, and a war between them started. Latinus died in the war, but Aeneas and the Latins won. He is said to be the father of our people."

"There is a little more to the story," added Remus. "The mother of Aeneas was the goddess Venus. When Aeneas died, she asked Jupiter to make him one of the immortals, and he became a god."

"I have always wondered about something," said Anna. "Why are we called Latins and not Trojans or Dardanians? They are the city and region where Aeneas came from."

"That is the part of the story that some people have forgotten today," responded Remus. "The goddess Juno was the protector of the Latin people, and she still is today. When Aeneas defeated Turnus, she was concerned that he would change our ancient name. She begged Jupiter to allow us, the Latins, to keep our name, our language, and our customs. Among other reasons, this is why we are so faithful to her."

During the telling of this story, Nivea sat beside me and was very attentive. She seemed to be hanging on every word as if she knew what we were saying. After the story, she walked from person to person, nudging each one of us gently with her head.

We chatted for a while longer, and then Gaius stood up, stretched, and voiced the question all of us had been considering silently: "What do we do now?"

Romulus answered quickly, as if he had been pondering the same question. "I think we should stay with the plan we had before. If we head north and east across the mountains, we will come to the land of the Umbrians. They are friendly toward our people, and we have no place else to go."

"I am not exactly sure how to get to one of the Umbrian villages from here," said Milo, "but I can guide us to their region. We should have no problem finding food along the way because the area is rich with fruit trees, game, and fish. Water could be a problem because we have nothing in which to carry it. We will have to drink what we can when we come to a stream, spring, or lake."

"Then let's get going," insisted Remus. "We don't know what the Vulci are planning, and the farther we are from them, the better I will feel."

Before leaving, we tried to cover up any evidence that we had been in the spot where we ate, including dispersing the remains of our fire. We also walked in different directions before coming together some distance away. It was important that we leave few traces so the Vulci could not track us if they came this way.

There were no trails for us to follow here, but luckily, the terrain included a mix of forests and open fields. We were able to make our way along animal trails. As we traveled we looked for more or less straight sticks and sharp rocks that would serve as weapons if we were attacked. With the rocks, we sharpened the sticks. Because of the cool and clear weather, we made good time. Nivea was a considerable help, too, because she seemed to be able to spot a trail when the rest of us could not.

We had no trouble finding either food or

water. At night, we looked for protected areas near trees, shrubs, or overhanging cliffs. The land was pleasant, but knowing how close the Vulci and the Arroni were, we recognized that it was not suitable for our home.

The hills became steeper and rockier as we moved farther east. We had to slow down considerably and rest more often. In some places we had to change direction entirely. There was also something unsettling about the area. A sulfurous scent floated through the air occasionally, and we could see what looked like smoke rising from springs in the distance.

"There are passages to the Underworld here," explained Milo. "They are not as big as those near Vesuvius, and the ground does not shake very often. The Etruscans believe that Vanth leads souls to the Underworld through these passages."

"Let's hope that she has no interest in us," prayed Romulus.

The trail led us into a canyon with steep, rocky walls. We realized it might be a box canyon, one with no outlet, but we had encountered these before. The only choice we had was to walk as far as we could and see what happened. If there was no way out, we would retrace our steps and find another trail. Nivea was not reluctant to enter the canyon, and we trusted her judgment.

When we were deep in the canyon, moving shadows fell upon us. Katia was the first to notice, and as she looked up, she said, "Those birds must be enormous. I've never seen anything like them."

"Nor have I," added Milo, with a touch of worry in this voice. "Some of the birds I have seen over the sea have a broad wing span, but none are as large as these."

Something about the shadows was eerie, and we hurried along a little faster. Our fears were well founded, and in a moment, what we thought were birds came swooping down shrieking loudly. Three Harpies, winged spirits known for their cruelty, were attacking.

Even if we had real weapons, we probably could not have defended ourselves well against these monsters. They are among the most bizarre of supernatural demons, with the face of a girl, slashing claws, and foul stench. They dove at us again and again, grabbing at us with their talons.

The canyon here offered no place to hide, so we ran to the rocky wall on one side and stayed as close to it as we could. At least in this position, the Harpies could come at us from only one direction. We pushed the youngest of our group behind us and jabbed at the beasts with our sharpened sticks. With each passing moment, their attack became more vicious.

"Stay as close to the ground as you can!" shouted Milo. "Keep your sticks pointed at the sky. The Harpies will not be able to reach us. And don't let them scratch you. An injury from their claws will fester terribly. Whatever it is that makes them stink is like poison to humans."

Crouched together on the ground, we held the sharpened sticks as Milo had directed. The Harpies could not reach us, but that did not deter them from trying. Their strategy soon changed, and they did something unforeseen. They grabbed the sticks and pulled them away from us one at a time. We would soon have no way to protect ourselves.

The Harpies are thieves at heart, we all knew. They liked to torture people by stealing everything from them, including their food. Eventually, those they torment die of starvation, and the Harpies carry their souls to the Underworld.

We had nothing for them to steal, but they were relentless in their attack. The scent of the Harpies was really disgusting, and their claws looked like they could pluck the limbs from our bodies. Romulus tried throwing stones at them, but the Harpies just shrieked with laughter at his effort.

Nivea, who had been growling and barking at the Harpies, turned her head to the sky and released a chilling wail. Echoing through the canyon, her baying startled the Harpies, who ceased their attack for a moment. At the same time, a mist drifted into the canyon and concealed us. The screams of the Harpies diminished, and we lost sight of them. The sound of their beating wings became softer, which meant that they were flying away.

For a few minutes, we didn't move or speak, so great was our fear. The mist was incredibly thick, and we could see almost nothing. Its chill pierced our clothing and muffled every sound. Within the mist, time seemed to stop, and we were alone in the world.

"Has anyone been injured?" asked Romulus.

"I don't think so," answered Gaius, who moved among us to make sure we were all present.

"We are against the left wall of the canyon," whispered Remus, "so we know our direction of travel. Do you think we should keep going through the fog?"

"Probably not," said Romulus. "We don't know what lies ahead of us, and it will be too easy to get separated. Leaving the canyon the way we came in makes no sense because we don't know how far the mist has spread. All we can do is stay here."

The cold and damp silence surrounded us. We could not even make a fire because there was nothing nearby that could be burned, and we were not willing to leave our position to search for wood. We resigned ourselves to doing nothing, when the mist that surrounded us began to swirl. A shadowy figure materialized, the same wraith that had caused the soldiers of Vulci to panic.

Chapter XV

The descent of Aeneas to Earth infuriated Discordia, who had recruited the Harpies to threaten the Albans. She complained to Jupiter that Aeneas, a former mortal, had interfered in the plans of a god. Jupiter, the king of the gods, pointed out that Aeneas had not interfered directly, but had simply appeared to the humans.

At the same time, the Keres were becoming irritated with Discordia. They believed that she should not have sent the Harpies to harass the Albans. More than anything else, the Keres wanted to feed on these humans.

We felt no panic as the shape drew near. It might have been because Nivea showed no aggression toward it. In fact, she sat as if she were waiting for a friend and then bolted toward the shape when it got close. Both she and the shape were enveloped in a bright light that warmed us before fading. Nivea returned, along with the shadow, which began to change and assumed the form of a person. It spoke to us in a voice that reached into our souls.

"Do not be afraid, my children. I am your ancestor Aeneas."

For whatever reason, the words of this apparition struck us as being true. Our reaction to what he said was immediate. The sense of *pietas* that we had learned since birth caused us to fall to our knees and bow our heads.

"Please, rise and let me look at you," he continued. "I have seen you from afar, but I wish to have the pleasure of knowing you better."

He approached each of us, touching us on the shoulder and smiling. When he came to Milo, he performed a different kind of greeting. He held his hand out to Milo, who did the same, and the two of them grasped forearms.

"You are a descendent of the Greeks who defeated us at Troy," said Aeneas. "Your people were brave and clever. You have grown powerful, and you have brought the knowledge of many things to the Latins and Etruscans. It gladdens me that you have risked your life to help this group of Albans. I can promise you that your deeds will not be forgotten."

"Was it you who brought the mist that drove off the Harpies?" I asked.

"One who is more honored than I am did that," he answered, and his hand stroked Nivea's head. "You will learn more about your special protector in the course of time. For now, I would like to show you something. Come with me, and do not be alarmed, no matter what you see."

Aeneas turned and walked through the mist, which parted as he progressed. We followed behind him, uncertain where we were going, but confident that he would not lead us astray.

Through the mist, we could see a dark lake and shadowy woods. Passing them by, Aeneas brought us to a cave, and explained that it would take us through the mountains. We could not travel through the cave alone, however, for it was also one of the entrances to the Underworld. He would guide us to be sure that we did not lose our way, for as he put it, "The path to the Underworld is easy, but to retrace your steps to the world of the living is a nearly impossible undertaking."

The entrance to the cave was small, but it widened as we walked downward. Coming around a turn, we caught our breath. The inside extended as far as we could see. In the distance were rivers, and we had little doubt what they were. These were the rivers that divided the world of the living from the Underworld. Charon the ferryman was hard at work transporting souls, and Cerberus, the three-headed watchdog of the Underworld, bayed monstrously. Despite Aeneas telling us that we should not be afraid, we were all terrified.

In a quiet voice, Romulus addressed our

guide. "Honored Aeneas, may I ask why you have brought us here? Given all you know, there must have been other ways through the mountains."

"It is a fair and thoughtful question," answered Aeneas. "You have all been loyal to the gods, and because of Discordia, you have suffered. I can also tell you that your trials have not yet been completed. The most troublesome challenges lie ahead for some of you. I wanted you to know that the Underworld was not just a story told to young people, and that the Fields of Elysium are waiting for those mortals who live a brave and righteous life."

"Can you tell us who will be among the challenged?" asked Remus.

"I am forbidden from telling you the future in such detail. If I did, you might try to change what lies ahead, or worse yet, do nothing and assume that you are predestined to succeed or fail. Your fate is what you make of it. And if you and your descendants achieve greatness, there is something I want you to remember. Crown peace with law, and spare those whom you conquer."

"Those are noble words," agreed Romulus, "but we are hardly in a position to make laws or conquer anyone. We have stumbled from one misfortune to another, and our prospects are bleak. Nonetheless, if we ever manage to settle into a normal life, we will heed your words."

As we made our way through this desolate place, Aeneas pointed to a trail that wound through the Underworld."See where the path splits in two? On one side is the way to Tartarus, where the wicked will spend eternity. The other path leads to Elysium, where the just souls remain until the cycle of time is complete."

We walked in silence, not straying for a moment from our guide. The shrieking of the souls condemned to suffer for all eternity was chilling, and we could see the demons and phantoms of our childhood stories flitting about. Whenever one of them drifted our way, a growl from Nivea sent it back to the other side.

Turning away from the vast cavern, Aeneas led us through a narrow opening. The ground sloped gently upward, and the path ahead of us was a little brighter, suggesting an opening. We emerged from the cave into the daylight on the far side of the steep hills through which we had been struggling before the Harpies attacked us. It was a relief to see the sky and to put the Underworld behind us.

"I will leave you here," said Aeneas, "but before you go, I have a small gift for you. It can be found in a cache behind the pile of stones over there."

Romulus and Remus removed the stones to which Aeneas was pointing. An ancient wooden box was nestled in a hole in the cliff. They removed it carefully, and from the way they carried it, we could see it was heavy. When they lifted the top, we saw what was inside. There were weapons made of iron that must have been hundreds of years old. They were a little rusty, but otherwise they were in perfect condition.

"These weapons were forged by Vulcanus on a far-off island and brought here by my people on our long journey. It is only fitting for you, who have also traveled so far, to have them."

Aeneas bid us farewell, saying something I will always remember: "Do worthy things." He brushed his hand down Nivea's back, and before our eyes, faded into a rising mist. Aeneas held his hand high to salute us, and we did the same. From that day onward, our people have always used this salute as both a greeting and a farewell to honor Aeneas.

"Does this place look familiar?" Chiara asked Milo.

"Not really, but the tall mountain to the northwest is the same one we noticed a few days ago. Given our travels since then and the position of the mountain, I think we are on the eastern frontier of the Vulci near the land of the Umbrians. I can climb to the top of the hill over there and get a better look at the land."

The hill to which he referred was south of the place where we stood. We all walked with him, for there was no longer any reason for us to stay by the mouth of the cave.

Milo and Remus climbed to the top of the hill. The rest of us picked fruit from the trees that grew around the base of the hill. For now, that was all we would eat. Once we had time to mount on shafts the spear heads that Aeneas gave us, we would be able to hunt the large animals that lived in the area.

"I wonder how long we were in the cave?" asked Nico.

"A few hours," answered Chiara, but then she hesitated. "You know, I'm not sure. I lost track of time, and I'm not even sure when we entered the cave."

"It is late afternoon now," said Nico, "because the sun is low in the western sky. There is no day or night in the Underworld, so there is no time. We have no idea how much time passed in the outside world."

"Look at the trees," said Chiara. "They still have their leaves and fruit. That means we could not have been in the Underworld for too long or the leaves would have fallen. But Nico is right in saying that we don't know if we are in the same day it was when the Harpies attacked."

Our talk about the time was interrupted by the return of Milo and Remus. They explained that we were north of a large lake that Milo knew. Onc of the Etruscan cities, Velzna, was near the lake. The Umbrian cities were a little farther to the east. Milo drew a map on the ground showing us where we were and which hills we could use as landmarks, depending on what we wanted to do.

"For tonight, we should probably camp here,"

suggested Romulus. "This spot has food and water, wood for a fire, and a small cave for shelter tonight. We can discuss what we will do tomorrow."

After building a fire near the mouth of the cave, we asked Milo about the Umbrians and the Velznans. He explained that he and the other Greeks had traded with both tribes, and that they also traded with Alba Longa. He had visited both groups in the spring and had found them to be fair and successful. We could reach Velzna in a day or two, and an Umbrian settlement in three or four days.

"Couldn't we just stay here and make this our home?" asked Katia. "It has everything that we need."

"As appealing as this idea is, I doubt that we can do it," explained Romulus. "We are still in the land of the Vulci, and we don't know how they would react to us after their revolt. The Arroni are not far away. One of these groups would undoubtedly discover us. Winter will soon be here, and I'm not sure we have enough time to build adequate shelters and gather all the food we need."

Looking back at the place where Aeneas had left us, Katia added, "Being this close to an entrance to the Underworld is more than I could bear. I could never sleep, knowing what is inside the cave."

"For now, at least, we will have to find a group

that will accept us," said Remus. "As part of a larger group, our chances of survival are better. Some day, we may find a place where we can start a new village."

We kept the fire burning brightly that night, and our weapons were at our sides. Although we took turns serving as guards and Nivea paced around us all night, the nearby presence of the entrance to the Underworld was creepy. What was even more terrifying was the howling of an animal in the distance.

All of us had heard wolves before. They were as much a part of our lives as the other wild animals in our home region. Some of us even enjoyed the wolf song that they made when they were together. This animal, however, was not a wolf.

The baying of the animal near our camp had a quality that sounded like a mix of wolf song and human wailing. Moreover, this creature howled even though it was alone, which wolves in our region never did. None of us slept well that night, and we were grateful when the morning sun brought silence to whatever beast we had heard.

Chapter XVI

When she becomes angry, Discordia's snaky hair writhes, and the ribbons entangled in it drip blood. This was precisely what happened as she watched the Albans sleeping after their passage through the Underworld.

She pushed the Keres aside as she paced back and forth. They were no help to her now because they only fed on the souls of the dead, not the living. She needed another way to assail them.

The partner she chose was a dreadful fiend, one that the Albans would not be prepared for. This beast would do what the Keres could not.

A dismal rain began to fall before the sun rose. I was on guard duty with Gaius and Nivea, so we moved from our position outside to the edge of the overhang. The noise of the falling rain woke the others, who grumbled about the weather. The cold and damp made sleeping out of the question, so we threw more wood on the fire to keep all of us warm.

"We have been lucky about the weather up until now," said Chiara. "Not many days have been this miserable. Do we want to continue our journey in this rain?"

"There's no reason for us to go anywhere," insisted Romulus. "We are dry and more or less warm here. We can put some wood beside the fire to dry so we have fuel for the rest of the day and tonight, if it keeps raining."

"Does anyone want to go hunting?" asked Chiara. "I'm tired of eating just fruit and nuts, and if Nivea catches a small animal, she refuses to share it with me."

Hearing her name, Nivea pranced over to Chiara, who sat down beside her. Chiara hugged the great dog and tickled her ears, which Nivea loved.

Gaius smiled and answered, "The old Chiara has returned. Since your kidnapping, you have been quiet and passive. I like having the old Chiara back. I'll bet Milo does, too."

We all laughed at the comment Gaius had made, but he was right. This was the first time that Chiara had acted with the boldness and humor that she had always shown. The change was something we all enjoyed.

"Back to my question," she said insistently. "Does anyone want to go hunting with me?"

"I doubt that any animals will be wandering

around at this hour and in this weather, but you would never speak to me again if I refused your offer," said Milo.

The two of them plodded off through the rain and disappeared from sight. By now, dawn was breaking, but the rain showed no sign of relenting.

Chiara and Milo returned about an hour later, soaked and empty-handed, but in good humor. They laughingly admitted that their hunting adventure was not a very good idea. They had seen no prey of any kind, and the only evidence of an animal was a set of peculiar footprints not far from our shelter. The one bit of good news they had was that the rains had brought out the land snails, and there were dozens of them clinging to a stone cliff not far from us. Because they were already wet, Milo and Chiara volunteered to collect these treats. Snails were one of our prized delicacies, and eating them would improve our mood on a dreary day.

Because we had nothing suitable to carry the snails, they made several trips, carrying what they could in their hands. We also had nothing in which to cook the snails, so we arranged them close to the fire. None of us had ever tried cooking them in this manner, and we were not sure how well it would work. The scent of the snails roasting was wonderful, and we were hopeful that they would taste as good as they smelled.

When Milo and Chiara returned after their final trip, Remus said with a smile, "We should let our accomplished hunters try the snails first. Their skill made this meal possible."

The joke brought laughs as well as agreement from Chiara and Milo, who quickly pulled a few snails from the fire and cracked the shells between rocks. They described the taste of the snails as fabulous, and the rest of us joined them in a tasty breakfast.

"If we ever chance upon any of my friends from Greece, just don't call me Snail Hunter," begged Milo. "They will carry the name back to my homeland, and I will be known by that title for the rest of my life."

The rain lasted for most of the day. In the afternoon, it finally stopped, and we decided to leave our shelter and go as far as we could in the direction of Velzna. We thought that given the weather, the nearer of our two possibilities made sense. Even though it was late in the day, we set off, hoping we could find decent shelter for the night.

Because we were at the far border of the area controlled by the Vulci, we felt safe traveling on a road that headed toward Velzna. It was muddy, but we made good time. Late in the day, we began looking for shelter for the night, and could not believe our luck. From the top of a hill, Gaius had spotted what he thought might be a necropolis. Believing that there could be incomplete tombs or shelters near the necropolis, we hurried in that direction.

What we found when we arrived at the building was puzzling. It was not a necropolis, but an incredible villa, the biggest home any of us had ever seen. Even Milo was impressed and claimed that this structure was larger and more elegant than any he had ever seen in Greece, his native land.

Equally surprising was that no one seemed to be around. In every case on our journey thus far, we had encountered armed people whenever we came to buildings. Although this villa was maintained well, no people could be seen.

"Given the time of day and the weather, I think we should go to the house and announce ourselves," suggested Gaius. Sighing, he added, "Nothing would please me more than spending a night in such a residence."

Although we agreed with the sentiment Gaius expressed, we were more reluctant to approach the villa than he was. Something was not right with such a magnificent home being here in the middle of a desolate area far from other dwellings. Nonetheless, we followed him to the door.

The villa consisted of several buildings made of large stone blocks. A wall enclosed a garden or other area behind the villa. Pillars supported a portico over the main door, and in many ways, the home resembled one of the elegant tombs in Tarquinii. The most stunning building to us was a small outbuilding with a round roof. We could not imagine how such a roof could remain in place, especially because other Etruscans had not figured out how to do it.

The huge front door creaked open. We were completely unprepared for this, so we took several steps back and drew our weapons. A well-dressed man appeared in the open doorway and looked at us. He said nothing and seemed unconcerned, although he stared at Nivea in a disturbing way. At the time, I thought he was being cautious of an unfamiliar dog.

"Forgive us," said Milo in the Etruscan language. "We are travelers on our way to Velzna. We are looking for a place to spend the night. We do not wish to intrude on you, and would be grateful if you would let us sleep in one of your far buildings."

"From your speech and clothing, I doubt you are Etruscan. It is likely that you are Greeks or Latins."

Taken aback by this response, Milo answered, "I am a Greek, and the rest of us are Latins."

"Then we can speak in the Latin language," said the man in our language. "My name is Lycus. Come into my home. I do not often have visitors here."

We entered the house cautiously. Nivea would not come with us. She paced outside, but did not try to stop us. Behaving like this was unusual but not unheard of. On some occasions, she has assumed a watchful position rather than staying with Romulus or Remus. From inside the house, I could see her through a *fenestra*, an opening in a wall that allowed light into the house. She sat where she could see us inside the house.

The inside of the house was breathtaking. The walls were painted with beautiful yet mysterious images. Statues were here and there, some of which were representations of humans, while others had an exaggerated length that was odd yet pleasing. The pottery that was placed about the room had intricate designs that told the stories of the gods. The wealth that it must have taken to build and furnish the house was unimaginable.

"You must be hungry," said Lycus. "There is plenty to eat in the *coquina*, the room where food is prepared. I have no fresh meat, but there is smoked meat, cheese, bread, and fruit."

None of us, with the exception of Milo, had ever seen a room dedicated to the preparation of food. In our homes, there was only one room, and part of it was used for eating. The room that Lycus brought us to was bigger than any building in our village. It had a fireplace for cooking, tables, chairs, and space for storage.

"Don't be shy. Help yourselves," said Lycus. "You all look very hungry."

At first, we politely picked at the food spread on the table, but in a moment, our hunger got the best of us, and we ate enthusiastically. This was the best meal we had eaten since the beginning of our journey. What was particularly delicious was the beverage that we had, a juice of some kind that we had never tasted before. Lycus watched us carefully and made sure that all of us drank it.

"Lycus, do you live here alone?" asked Nico. "Your home is so large and beautiful that our whole village could live in it."

"I have a few people who help me, but otherwise, I live here alone. My helpers are not here today. Maybe you will meet them before you leave."

"Are you affiliated with one of the Etruscan tribes?" asked Romulus. "You must have difficulty protecting yourself on this frontier."

"The Etruscans and other tribes have chosen to allow me to live here in peace," answered Lycus. "They rarely come this way, and when they do, they keep a respectful distance."

"You are more fortunate than we have been," said Romulus. "Some of the Etruscan tribes have been bent on our destruction, and even the forces of nature oppose us. Despite our adversities, however, we have managed to survive."

"Well," said Lycus, "I hope that our meeting marks a change in your fortunes."

Although I was as pleased as the others that we had food and a place to spend the night, something was just not right about Lycus and his surroundings. Even his wishing us well had a sinister tone. Had they chosen to, the Etruscans could easily overpower him and occupy this villa, yet they did not. Dozens of servants would be needed to maintain these buildings, but there was no one else around. With an entrance to the Underworld just a short distance away, I became curious about this strange man.

"Who built this house for you?" asked Katia. "They were very talented, and moving the blocks of stone must have been quite a feat."

"We can talk about that another time," answered Lycus. "You are probably weary after being outside in such weather. Follow me, and I will show you where you can sleep."

Lycus brought us to a large room with a fireplace. It was warm and had comfortable furnishings. He told us that we could spend the night there and turned to leave. Before he did, Gaius spoke to him.

"I have a question, Lycus, and I hope you won't think badly of me. How can a person afford such a home?"

"It is a long story, and I am sure that you have had enough of my ramblings," he answered. "Living alone, I sometimes go on and on when guests are here."

With that, Lycus left us, closing the door behind him. No sooner had he departed than all of us fell fast asleep.

Chapter XVII

While the Albans slept, Discordia appeared to Lycus. He thanked her for bringing the Albans to him, and she was grateful that Lycus had come up with such a dreadful plan for them.

Lycus was a shapeshifter, a being who could change his appearance and cause others to change. For now, he alternated between human form and that of a beast that looked like a wolf but walked on two legs. The fate he had in mind for the Albans was in many ways worse than death and would affect anyone who had the misfortune to encounter them.

My sleep was fitful, filled with dreams of the horrid things I had seen in the Underworld. I opened my eyes and saw that the others were awakening, too. The place was dark except for a ghostly light near the center of the room. In this light stood Lycus.

Instead of the person we had met, Lycus changed from one form to another. At one moment he was a human, and at the next, a wolf-like beast that sneered at us. We grabbed for our weapons, but he laughed at us because our movements were so clumsy.

"Your weapons cannot harm me in any form I take. I am hundreds of years old and have survived greater threats than you. I was once a human, but I chose immortality by pledging myself to Calusna and allowing one of his minions to bite me. Now I spread the curse of transformation among humans, and you will help me."

Looking at Romulus, he added, "You asked before about how I protect myself from the Etruscans and the other tribes. They fear me and almost never come to this region, and they know that an entrance to the Underworld is nearby. Only foolish or naïve people like you would ever find themselves in my realm."

It was only then that we realized that we could not take hold of our weapons. We moved at a sluggish pace as if time had slowed down. We were under the spell of Lycus and were powerless.

"You are probably wondering what I have planned for you," smirked Lycus. "I am happy to explain. With just a small bite from me, you will all become shapeshifters and merge your human form with that of a wolf. Because you did not choose this fate, it will be out of your control. When you change shapes, you will attack other humans, who in turn will become infected. You will cause fear and dread on an enormous scale, and the whole time, you will have no idea what happened."

"I would end my life before doing such things," shouted Romulus.

"You will have no knowledge of what you did," insisted Lycus. "The drink I gave you earlier this evening is laced with water from the River Lethe, and you will forget everything about this night and what you do in the future as shapeshifters. The gods will know, as will I, but you will be oblivious."

Lycus turned to Nico, who sat unable to move in the spot where he had slept. A look of dread was on his face, and none of us could help him. At that instant, Nivea leaped through the *fenestra* closest to Lycus. Her leap startled him, and he turned quickly and snarled at her.

Nivea seemed to be no match for Lycus in his beastly form. Even though she was a large dog, he towered over her in his wolfish shape. She growled and snapped at him, and as she did, the room seemed to glow. Perhaps because he was so intent on Nivea, for a moment, we were out of his spell.

Romulus, who had been struggling to get to his feet, suddenly stood up. He reached into his tunic and pulled out the silver knife that he had picked up in Vulci. He rushed forward, threw himself at Lycus, and stabbed him in the heart, jumping back quickly so as not to let the beast's foul blood touch him. Romulus stumbled, fell over backward, and lay motionless on the ground.

We all remembered that Lycus said our weapons were useless against him, and he tried to pluck the knife from his chest. When he touched the silver knife, however, it glowed with an unearthly light, which spread to all parts of his body. He howled in an agonizing voice, and a moment later, he fell to the floor. Both he and the silver knife vanished, as did the building around us. We found ourselves standing in an open field in the middle of the night with only faint moonlight for illumination.

"What happened?" asked Romulus, sitting up and rubbing the back of his head.

Rushing to his side, Remus answered, "Lycus and his house simply vanished. Are you all right?"

"I'm fine," said Romulus. "I remember stabbing Lycus and trying to avoid his blood, but I lost my balance when I did."

"Everything we saw must have been caused by Lycus the shapeshifter," murmured Milo. "With his powers, he was able to create his villa out of nothingness. I have heard of such things, but I never thought they were true."

"But the food we ate must have been real," insisted Chiara. "I remember being hungry and then feeling full after I ate. And it tasted good."

"Even that was probably magical," said Remus. "Look around where the house was. Nothing is left other than what we brought with us."

"Had it not been for Nivea, we would be in a horrible situation," I whispered, stroking the dog's head. "Can you imagine how awful it would be to hurt innocent people, including our own friends and family, and not even know what we were doing?"

A small grove of trees was nearby, and we thought about spending the night there. We started a fire and hoped it wouldn't rain. Between the damp ground and the memory of what happened with Lycus, none of us could sleep. Before long, we decided to continue our journey to Velzna. We would not travel very quickly, but we wanted to escape this cursed place as soon as we could.

As we walked, Milo told us about what we should expect. We couldn't see because even the scant moonlight was being blocked by an increasing cover of clouds.

"The road we are on is more or less flat with rolling hills. It is not used very often by the Etruscans because their cities are mostly along the coast. The Umbrians also use the road, but their settlements are to the east. There is a river nearby, and on both sides of us are hills, some of which are tall and steep."

"Do you think that there are areas along this road where we might settle?" asked Romulus.

"I'm not sure," answered Milo. "The area is not populated by many people, and it has water and good soil. Neither the Etruscans nor the Umbrians have a strong presence here. Nonetheless, both tribes claim the region. We will have a better idea about this possibility after we reach Velzna."

The sky was beginning to lighten, and we were relieved that dawn would soon be here. The weather, however, did not cooperate, and the rain started falling. We were miserable.

We passed a rocky outcropping, went up a small hill, and descended into a valley. A slight smell of sulfur reached us, reminding me of Vesuvius. Milo, however, seemed unconcerned, although he picked up the pace a little.

"I know you all smell the sulfur in the air," he insisted, "but don't worry. This isn't like Vesuvius, and I think you will be happy about what we find."

A few minutes later, he took us off the road on a small path. The path ended at a rock formation beside a pool of water from which smoke was arising. The smell of sulfur became stronger, but the air around the pool was warm. The rocks beside the pool were relatively soft, and it appeared as if humans had cut a small shelter into the rock. In this shelter, we were protected from the rain, and because of the heat from the pool, we were warm.

"This is a sacred spring," explained Milo, "a gift to humans from the goddess Aegeria. It is said to have healing powers."

"I don't know about the healing powers," said Chiara, "but the warming powers of the spring are more important now."

With that, Chiara removed her outer garments and slid into the pool. The rest of us followed her example, and the warm water felt incredible. The only exception was Romulus, who collected wood and started a fire. Once it was blazing, he put our clothes around the fire to dry before joining us.

Nivea walked to the far edge of the pool and stepped in gingerly. She settled into the water up to her neck and let out a sigh of satisfaction. Then she stood up and shook her fur. After sending a spray of water all over us, she plopped down beside the fire.

We used the excuse of waiting for our clothes to dry so we could stay in the warm water. Eventually, hunger got the best of us, and we left the spring. We stood between the fire and the warm spring until we were dry. Our undergarments were still wet, but we were so used to damp clothes that we finished dressing and then went on a hunt. We were lucky and found a herd of deer nearby. With so many of us, it was not difficult to surround the herd and bring one of them down with a spear.

While Remus and I skinned and gutted the deer, the others gathered fruit and nuts. We carried the carcass back to the fire and suspended it over the flames with our spears. Given our hunger, it was difficult to wait until the deer was cooked thoroughly. Each of us cut off a small piece of the deer and held it over the fire on the tip of a knife. This snack plus some fruit held us over until the whole deer was cooked.

By the time we ate, it was midday, and the weather had improved. The sky was clear, so we set off once again for Velzna. All of us carried enough fruit and cooked meat to last for two days, the time it would take for us to reach our destination.

The remainder of our journey was routine. From the crest of a hill, Milo pointed out Velzna on the edge of a huge lake, the largest we had ever seen. The city was not as large as the other Etruscan cities we had seen, but it was far bigger than our village. Not long after we caught a glimpse of the city, several riders intercepted us on the road. They were armed and cautious but not aggressive.

"We wish you a good day," said Milo in the language of the Etruscans. "We are travelers on our way to Velzna. May we enter the city?"

"You speak our language, but you are not of our people. Who are you?" asked one of the men.

"My name is Milo, and I am a Greek who has traded with your people. These young people are Latins from Alba Longa."

"You look familiar," said another of the men. "I recognize you from the meetings where we exchange goods. I am one of the guards, so we have never spoken. Come with us, and we will escort you to the city."

The riders chatted with us as we walked. One of them said, "We were surprised when we saw you on the road. Very few travelers use this road north of Velzna."

Romulus did something clever at that point, hoping to learn what the guards knew about Lycus. He asked, "Why do you think that is?"

The guards looked at each other before one of them answered. "Strange things have happened on the road farther north. Our people almost never go beyond the sacred spring. Some people say there is an entrance to the Underworld, while others claim there is a mysterious creature that lives in a huge villa."

Understanding what Romulus was doing, Milo quickly added, "We crossed over from Tarquinii using the trail that joins the road near the spring."

Speaking softly to us so the armed men could not hear, Milo warned us to say nothing about what we had gone through. If the people of Velzna thought that we had contact with Lycus or had passed through the Underworld, they would suspect us of sorcery. They would undoubtedly refuse to let us into the city, or worse, harm us.

Chapter XVIII

Discordia could not decide what bothered her most, seeing Lycus destroyed by an Alban teenager or dealing with humiliation at the hands of the other gods. She complained to Jupiter about interference by Juno, but the king of the gods pointed out that Romulus killed Lycus without help, using a knife that was made by her allies, the Vulci.

Realizing that the Albans were far more resilient than she had anticipated, Discordia decided to enlist an unusual ally. The giant Enceladus had been buried under a volcano called Etna far away on the island of Sicania. He might be able to help in an unexpected way.

The horsemen led us into the city, and the people of Velzna paid little attention to us. Some smiled and greeted us politely, and we felt welcome. Several people called to Milo by name, which made us feel comfortable.

On a small street near a large square, the riders dismounted. They led us by foot to a shelter with open sides and a roof. Several men and women sat in the shelter, and they rose when we approached them. They seemed to be leaders of some kind, based on their clothes and the way the horsemen spoke to them.

"Milo, we haven't seen you in ages," said one of the men.

"Talitus, my friend, it is good to see you," answered Milo in the Etruscan language. He clasped the older man's hand and put his other hand on the man's shoulder. He bowed his head slightly, as did Talitus. Their respect for one another was obvious from their gestures.

Although we understood a little of the Etruscan language, Milo repeated in our language everything that he or the Velznans said. He did so with great ease, and it was at that moment that I grasped how important it was to be versed in the languages of all the people in our land. I vowed at that moment to learn as much as I could of the Etruscan language and the other languages spoken by different tribes.

Turning to the others, Milo bowed his head and then spoke to one of the women. "You are as lovely as ever, Sethra. I wish I had a gift for the wife of my friend, but I have not been to my homeland, and I would not offer you something inferior."

The woman walked up to Milo and gave him a hug as a mother might hug a child. She was beautiful and distinguished, and the first thought that went through my mind was, "When I become a woman, I hope to be like her."

"Please introduce me to your friends," said Sethra, and she looked at us with a smile on her face.

Milo introduced us one at a time, and Sethra had something kind or clever to say about each of us in our own language. She fawned over Nivea, who whimpered with joy at making a new friend. It was as if Sethra was an aunt who had not seen us for years. Her greeting almost made me cry as I thought of my mother and the aunts I might never see again.

"So what brings you to our city?" asked Talitus.

Not knowing how much we should share, no one answered for a moment. Then Romulus stepped forward and said, "We are from a small village near Alba Longa. Because of drought and an attack by raiders, our village had to follow the tradition of sundering, as did the Lydians long ago. We are looking for a new home. We are hard workers and will be loyal to whoever gives us a chance to show what we can do."

"We have traded with the Albans for many years," said Talitus, "and we remain on good terms with them. There is plenty of land in our territory that is suitable for farming, and there are other ways that you can employ yourselves among us.

Our miners, metal workers, and potters are always looking for willing hands. Although we know little about you, if you are friends of Milo, we have confidence that we can trust you."

"Stop being so formal," insisted Sethra. "In the name of Voltumna, these are children who have been forced away from their home. Of course they will be welcome here, and we will do everything we can to help them. And you are not going to make them find a place outside the city walls. They are going to stay inside the walls and work in the fields like the others."

Voltumna, I learned later, was the most esteemed god of Velzna and the other Etruscan cities. Sethra had a special place in her heart for him and felt he was the protector of her city.

"My wife and I have three children of our own," sighed Talitus, "but that is not enough for her. She treats every child in the city as her own, and now she has adopted you. Come, we have shelters that we keep for traders and visiting workers. You can live there as long as you like until you are settled."

The shelters were not far from where we stood. As we made our way to them, it was difficult to believe that we were not dreaming. Sethra and Talitus spoke of the opportunities that awaited us, and when they saw several young people working in a market, they asked them to join us.

Pointing at some structures on the far side of

the market, Talitus said, "These are the quarters I mentioned. I hope they are acceptable."

The buildings were more than acceptable; they were bigger and more beautiful than any in our village or Alba Longa. The inside of the building that Sethra led us to had furniture, sleeping pads in one room, and even a *coquina* for cooking. We were completely speechless, but Chiara expressed our feelings when she rushed to Sethra and hugged her.

"You are probably hungry," insisted Talitus, "and I think we should get you some food before we send you out to the fields. We are in the middle of the harvest season, and your help will be indispensable." Smiling at his wife, he added, "Sethra, don't spoil them. The people of Alba Longa have a reputation for being good workers. If you dote over them too much, they will not live up to their reputation."

Two of the teenagers who had joined us ran back to the market with some coins that Talitus gave them. They returned shortly with fruit, bread, and cooked meat. We drank water from a spring that was in a small plaza between the buildings. It flowed into a stone trough and then through a channel to an opening in the wall. The springs in our village were less complicated, but we had seen similar arrangements in the other Etruscan cities.

Sethra and Talitus excused themselves and asked Milo to take us out to the fields after we finished eating. He knew the area around the city and the person who was supervising the workers. While we were eating, Remus asked Milo a question.

"How do the coins work? In our village and the other settlements around us, we simply trade goods. The Etruscans use coins for some of their transactions, but we don't understand it."

"Each of the Etruscan cities makes their own coins. We do it in Greece, too. The coins are equal in value to some goods. When Talitus wanted food for you, he did not have goods to trade. Instead, he gave Parthi and Tanaquil some coins that they used to buy food."

"What keeps people from making coins and buying things without having goods to back them up?" asked Chiara.

Milo held up a coin and said, "There is an image of the leader of the city on the coins. This one has a likeness of Sethra. The number of coins is counted carefully, and they are not easy to make. Even so, some people try to make and use coins. When they are caught, they are punished severely."

"Are you saying that Sethra is the leader of this city?" asked Chiara. Her tone of voice showed the surprise all of us felt. We had never known a tribe with a female leader.

"Sethra and Talitus are the two main leaders of Velzna," insisted Milo. "It is not unusual in some Etruscan cities for women and men to share the leadership role. That is very different from what we do in Greece, where all of our leaders are men. It is difficult for some traders to accept Sethra, but she has proven to be a great ruler and wise trader."

"Until this moment," said Chiara, "I had never dreamed that I or any woman could be the leader of a tribe." Looking at Milo, she laughed. "If I ever do become a leader, I will be happy to share the role with you."

"If that time ever comes, I will be honored to share leadership with you," answered Milo. "For the present, however, we should head out to the fields so you can see what work awaits us."

Parthi and Tanaquil, two of the young Velznans, joined us as we walked through one of the gates in the wall to the agricultural area beyond. Romulus stopped us for a moment to examine a channel of water that ran under the wall. It was the water from the spring near our shelter. He asked Parthi and Tanaquil about how it worked.

"The water from the springs and rainfall is carried out of the city through these little canals," explained Tanaquil. "Once it is outside of the city walls, it feeds into a larger canal. We use all this water to irrigate our plants."

She pointed to the network of canals in the agricultural area and continued. "This land used to be a huge marsh. There were many insects, and diseases somehow came from the marsh.

Many years ago, our people dug these canals and drained the land. We can now use the land to grow things, and the water flows into the Marta River."

"There is one more thing," said Parthi. "You can see the trees we planted around the fields, along the canals, and beside the river. They also absorb the water and keep the soil from washing away in storms. Sometimes we cut the trees down to use for building or to burn for fuel. We replace those we cut down with new trees." He seemed very proud about what his people had done to make this land useful.

The agricultural area had several sections. The largest were fields for beans and wheat. Beyond them were orchards of fruit and olive trees. Livestock were kept in large penned areas between the fields and the city wall. If there was an attack, cattle, goats, and other animals could be brought within the walls.

"My father is working in the olive grove," said Tanaquil. "If you want to start now, he would be happy to have you."

We were eager to help and followed Tanaquil to her father's group of trees. She explained who we were, and with Milo's help, he told us what he wanted us to do. None of us had ever picked olives in this way, but what he described was not difficult.

At home, because our trees were small, we could pick the olives by hand. The trees here were a little taller, so we used long sticks to knock the olives from the trees. A few of us collected the olives as they fell and put them in baskets.

"This is as far north as olives can be grown dependably," explained Milo. "The weather gets too cold farther north."

After our day of working together, Tanaquil and Parthi were like old friends. We learned more of the Etruscan language, and we could carry on conversations with them, as long as the topics were familiar to us. Despite our trust in them, we did not share all the details of our adventures thus far.

When we returned to the city, some other young people were waiting for us in our shelter, as was Sethra. They had prepared a meal for us and had even found some different clothes that we could wear. Sethra had a knack for knowing what would please us, and she brought special treats for Nivea.

The meal was delicious, and after we ate, some of the young people played music for us. Their instruments were much more ornate than what we were used to, and their dances were more intricate. We were a little embarrassed at first to join the dancers, but it was difficult to resist. All of us joined with partners from Velzna, except Milo and Chiara, who danced with one another.

Sethra lit candles and oil lamps, and their light made our living quarters even more beautiful. We hated to see the evening end, but Sethra said that we would have a busy day tomorrow. The young Velznans returned to their homes, Sethra left us, and we all fell asleep on the pads that had been provided for us. We were filled with hope that we had found our new home.

Chapter XIX

Leaving her cloud on Olympus, Discordia darted to Earth in a swift whirlwind. She reached the island of Sicania and descended into the depths of the volcano named Etna. As a goddess, she could not be harmed by the enormous heat of Etna that was so great it melted rocks.

The giant Enceladus was delighted to see her. He was rarely visited by any of the immortals since being condemned to this place for rebelling against the gods.

Knowing that Enceladus had no friends among the gods, Discordia pretended kindness and concern for him. In exchange for her interest, she asked just a small favor. She wanted him to travel through the Underworld to a far-away land and release his fearsome fire.

The next few days were filled with so much activity that we were almost overwhelmed. We made friends, found work, and began to build a new life. One of the most pleasant features was the joy of living beside a lake.

Parthi and Tanaquil taught us to swim well enough so that we could go out on a boat and help with the fishing. We found it so enjoyable that it hardly seemed like work, yet the fishermen we helped paid us with coins.

We had finished working one afternoon and were sitting on a dock before returning to the city for the evening meal. The ground shook slightly, and remembering our experience with Vesuvius, we jumped up in a panic.

"It is nothing," insisted Parthi. "The ground here shakes sometimes, and in some places, new hot springs form. We have gotten used to these rumblings, and in time, so will you."

"Perhaps we will," answered Romulus, "but until that time, I'll feel more comfortable being on firm ground and not a wooden dock."

The rest of us agreed with Romulus and walked off the dock onto the shore. Parthi and Tanaquil were teasing us about our fear of the tremors when the ground shook again, much stronger than before. The two of them and the other Velznans stopped what they were doing, as tremors this strong were rare.

The water in the lake began to boil. A huge explosion took place near the far shore, and a volcanic island was pushed up from the bottom of the lake. Moments later, a second explosion brought another island to the surface. From these two small volcanoes came fire and ash, along with a swarm of nightmarish beings from the Underworld.

None of us knew what to do, but Remus shouted, "Run to the city! We will be safer behind the walls!"

"No!" insisted Tanaquil. "Head toward the pasture. It's not safe to be near a building when the ground shakes."

Everyone who was near the lake ran to the open pasture. The shaking of the ground became worse, and the narrow road crumbled under our feet. In places all around us, the ground collapsed, and from these fissures escaped foul-smelling fumes.

We reached the pasture and were looking at the city when the strongest tremor of all knocked us to the ground. Then, in a matter of moments, the walls of Velzna collapsed, along with most of the buildings inside.

My first thought as I lay on the ground was that the people we had come to know so well had been killed. But a moment later, through the dust, they walked out of the destruction, shaken but mostly uninjured.

"How can that be?" asked Romulus. "No one could survive such a collapse."

Parthi said, "Whenever the ground starts to shake, we know to leave the buildings. That is why we have so many open spaces in the city."

Our relief that the people were safe was quickly replaced by terror. From the crevices in the ground caused by the tremors crept phantom warriors from the Underworld. Above us flew the vile spirits that had escaped from the volcanoes in the lake. The people of Velzna, stunned by the earthquake, faced a terrible fate.

All of us who had been at the lake, including the Velznans, had weapons. We were always armed when we left the city. Some of the people who had stumbled out of the city were also armed.

"Form a defensive line between the attackers and the people of Velzna," shouted Romulus. "Back up slowly so we can protect them."

We stood side by side with the Velznans and faced the attackers. Nivea stood between them and us growling and barking. She seemed to be no match for the creatures, but none of them came at her directly. Instead, they went far around her and came at us from the side.

"Milo, stay behind us and help us communicate with the Velznans," insisted Romulus. "We don't speak their language well enough. You do."

Although he was reluctant at first, Milo knew that Romulus was right. He turned to go, but before he did, he ran to Chiara and the two of them embraced.

Nico and Katia stood bravely beside Romulus and Remus. These two children seemed out of place, but they held their weapons and waited to be told what to do. It was heartbreaking to see them in such danger.

Looking around, Romulus saw that Talitus and Sethra were among the Velznans who were injured. They were sitting at the edge of a pile of rubble. Romulus saw an opportunity and said, "Nico and Katia, go to Talitus and Sethra. They are right behind you and seem to be injured. See if you can help them, and if nothing else, protect them."

Hesitant to leave the others, Katia said, "We want to stay here with you. We know how to fight."

"I know you do," insisted Romulus, "and that's why I want you to protect Talitus and Sethra."

The first wave of attackers came upon the Velznans on the far right. It was then that we discovered that the weapons the Velznan fighters had were useless against the demons from the Underworld. They were overrun in minutes, and it appeared as if the demons would slaughter us.

Gaius was closest to them, and the attackers came toward him, confident that his weapons would be just as harmless. What Gaius did to a demon gave us all hope. He jabbed at one of the flying creatures, and the moment his spear touched it, the demon uttered a horrible shriek and fell to the ground. It was only then that we saw that his weapons, as well as ours, glowed with a supernatural light.

Romulus knew at once what was going on because of his experience with Lycus. "The weapons of the Velznans are useless," he shouted. "Tell them to get behind us. If anyone has an extra weapon of any kind, give it to a Velznan. Our weapons were made by Vulcanus on Sicania, so they have the power to kill the demons."

We were not alone in noticing that our weapons were deadly to the phantoms. They changed their strategy and started to assault the Velznans. This gave us an opportunity to go on the attack against them. Even the slightest blow from one of our weapons would destroy the creatures.

By now, we had shared our weapons with many of the Velznans, and the tide of the battle had turned. None of the fiends from the Underworld had any fear of us, but their numbers had been reduced. They must have realized that they were losing this battle, so the demons redirected their attack to the Velznans who had survived the earthquake.

Nivea saw this and rushed to Talitus and Sethra. Nivea, Katia, and Nico held the phantoms at bay briefly, giving us enough time to regroup and charge them. The battle was fierce, and more of the Velznans died before we killed the last of the demons.

All of us, Albans and Velznans, clustered together around Talitus and Sethra. Thankfully, their injuries were not severe, nor were those of the other survivors. All of those who had been set upon by the demons, however, had perished. Even if they had just been injured, the venom of the Underworld creatures was enough to kill them.

"The sun is setting," said Talitus, "and we do not have time now to mourn our losses. We have to build fires and make temporary shelters where we can spend the night. There is probably food we can recover from the rubble. And we must thank the gods for sparing us." Looking at us, he added, "And for bringing the Albans to us. Without you, we would all have been doomed."

It was hard not to admire Talitus as he tried to struggle to his feet. After the grimmest of disasters, his first thoughts were for the safety of his people. Instead of cursing the gods for the misfortunes that had befallen us, he thanked them for our safety. And instead of blaming us, he expressed his gratitude for what we did.

The magnitude of the disaster hit us then for the first time. We had been with a relatively small group of Velznans near the shore of the lake. As fierce as the battle had been, only a hundred or so people had been involved. But now we could see that thousands of people had been left homeless.

"Let's make fires first," suggested Romulus. "The night will be cool, and the fires will keep us warm. They will also give us a place to gather. I think that being together will be important tonight."

I was standing beside Sethra, and I noticed how intently she looked at Romulus and listened to his words. Turning to me, she said, "He is special, isn't he?"

"He is," I agreed. "When we have time, I will tell you more about him."

Finding wood was not hard because so many structures had been damaged beyond repair. We simply pulled wood from the rubble and stacked it where we would build the fires. Talitus suggested making the fires in a row that would parallel where the city's wall had been standing. The ruins of the city would protect our back, and building the fires in this way would form a defensive position, if it became necessary.

We had no trouble starting the fires, because some of the city was already in flames. During the earthquake, cooking fires had ignited some fallen timbers. All we had to do was retrieve some burning embers from these fires.

Nivea led us to the places in the rubble where some caches of food could be found easily. It was lucky that she had such a good nose, because the destruction was such that the people of Velzna could not even recognize where the food storehouses or markets were. We were able to retrieve enough food for the thousands of people who would be spending the night by the fires.

Sethra and Talitus limped among their people huddled around the fires. They made sure that mothers with young children and the elders had enough food and were close to the fire. They supported as well as they could those who had lost loved ones in the disasters.

When the two of them returned, they joined us by our fire. They asked Milo to come over and interpret for them and us. With a tone of respect, Sethra said, "There is more to the story of your coming than you have told us. It is clear that you are an extraordinary group of young people. Even your dog has abilities that are not easily explained. We would like to know who you are."

The moment was tense, and we were not sure how to proceed. We trusted both Sethra and Talitus, but we were not sure how hearing our story would shape their opinion of us. Of greater importance was how the people of Velzna would feel when they eventually learned of our experiences.

Milo broke the silence and said, "Because I speak both the Etruscan and Latin languages, I will begin the story. But because I am not aware of everything that happened, I will ask each of you to fill in details as you saw them."

He began with our first meeting, and each of us added something to what he described. The Velznans who sat near us could not believe what they heard, and I have to admit that even though I lived through the adventure, it seemed almost unreal.

The story that we told through Milo circulated quickly among the rest of the Velznans.

Each of his statements was repeated by a listener, who then shared it with more people. Many of the details were eliminated, but through this story chain, the account of our ordeals was shared with the survivors.

When we finished, we waited for the reaction of Sethra and Talitus. Much to our relief, they expressed amazement rather than fear. Just as welcome were the murmurs of encouragement we heard from other Velznans. We were grateful that they still seemed to be favorable toward us, and we were aware of how lucky we were to have come to know them.

Chapter XX

The defeat of the forces of the Underworld by the humans caused an odd reaction in Discordia. She became angry with Enceladus, even though he had done exactly what she had asked. With shrieks and wails, she drove him back to Etna, swearing that he would spend all eternity alone under the mountain.

Distracted by her fury with Enceladus, Discordia paid no attention to the Albans and the Velznans. For a short time, at least, they might be able to live without her interference in their affairs.

In the morning light, the destruction of Velzna was even more terrible. There was virtually nothing about the city that could be salvaged. What made things worse was the Velznans' fear of further earthquakes and volcanic activity. Without question, they would have to abandon their city.

Part of the city wall was piled in a heap behind Talitus. Climbing up on the pile, the leader addressed his people. "As all of you can see, our city has been devastated. There is practically nothing that can be retrieved from the ruins because of the dangers involved in recovery. We are going to have to rebuild our city."

His words were, to us, unbelievable. First of all, what he was suggesting would involve a monumental effort. And second, he seemed far less distressed about the prospect than we would have expected. What he said next helped us understand his reaction better.

"As all of you know, we have established a defensive outpost about a day's distance from here near the Tiber River. More than a hundred of our people live on the flat summit of a hill. There are supplies of food there and building materials. I think we have no choice but to go there and make a new Velzna. I am determined that this new city will be even better than before."

A roar went up from the crowd, and we could not help but join their cheers. The people of Velzna were just as committed to rebuilding their city as Talitus was. They were undaunted by the challenge that faced them, and we would help them in any way that we could.

When the crowd settled down, Sethra made her way up the pile of stones. In a soft but firm voice, she said, "Before we set out, there are two tasks we have to undertake. One is to bury our dead, and the other is to offer a sacrifice to Voltumna for sparing the rest of us."

Surprisingly, the number of dead was less than thirty. In the heat of the battle, we had not realized how effective our weapons had been against the demons. At first, we thought that the Velznans would carry their dead to the necropolis adjacent to the city, but all of the tombs were already in use. Sethra had another idea. Using the stones from the collapsed walls and buildings of the city, she wanted to build a second necropolis against a nearby hillside.

There was no shortage of building materials, given how many stones there were. A small army of workers quickly formed. The tomb builders directed the construction, and in a matter of hours, a row of burial chambers was in place against the hill. The dead were respectfully arranged inside the chambers with the few goods their families could spare, and the tombs were sealed.

In gathering the bodies of the fallen Velznans, we made a startling discovery. There were no remains of the creatures of the Underworld. The only signs that they had ever existed were discolorations on the ground where each of them had perished. For the most part, these were unrecognizable, but in a few cases, the outline of the fallen beast could be seen on the ground. It was a chilling sight that we all tried unsuccessfully to erase from our memories.

After the dead had been laid to rest, the survivors assembled around the altar that had been built to Voltumna. Because it was away from the city and simply constructed, it had not been affected by the recent tremors. There was very little left to offer as a sacrifice, but Sethra had a practical solution.

The earthquake had not harmed the livestock grazing in the fields. Sethra had herders separate the finest sheep and bring them to the altar. There, the *haruspex* of the tribe sacrificed the sheep and removed the entrails: the inner organs. To the Etruscans, the *haruspex* possessed special powers to see the future from the insides of animals. The rest of each sheep was prepared for roasting. After it was cooked, the meat would be shared by the people of Velzna before they made the journey to the site of the new city.

While the sheep were roasting, the *haruspex* examined the insides that had been removed from the animals. His expression was intent, and to us, seemed worrisome. Seeing our faces, Sethra said, "Don't be alarmed. Aranth enters a trance when he examines the entrails of the animals."

Lifting his head, Aranth said something we could not anticipate. "Could someone bring the dog to me?"

Romulus, who had been standing near the fire where the sheep were roasting, brought Nivea over to Aranth. He knelt on the ground in front of her, held her head in his hands, and leaned his head against hers. Aranth stood up with a slight smile and spoke in a confident voice.

"The signs are very clear to me. Our new city will be successful, and the Albans will join us on our journey. But they will not stay with us. Their destiny is in another place, not far from our new home. A painful price will be paid, however. And the dog that has protected you for so long still has a special role in your fate."

The words of Aranth were both comforting and disturbing. What made them so believable was that they were similar to what Aeneas had said. But we wondered what price would be paid, and who would pay it.

After having their final meal at their old home, the Velznans recovered what they could from the ruins of their city. They worked carefully because the ground still shook occasionally, and the wreckage of the city was unstable. They were able to collect a little food, some clothes, a few weapons, and a handful of tools. These would be of importance to the creation of the new city.

When all was ready, Talitus lifted a copper disk suspended on a loop of twine. This ceremonial instrument had been rescued from one of the sacred sites in the city. He hit the gong once with a hammer made from the horn of a deer. The single note echoed through the ruins with an eerie sound, marking the end of one city and the beginning of another. When the sound died, we set off on our journey.

With thousands of people and herds of livestock, we made an imposing group. Our progress was slow but steady, and we stopped often to allow the animals to graze. On one of these stops, some of our friends left their families and joined us. This gave us an opportunity to learn more about our destination.

"Tanaquil, do you know where we are going?" asked Romulus.

"I've never been there, but the site of the outpost is northeast of the city." She paused and corrected herself. "That is, the old city."

"We know how you feel," said Remus. "Walking away from our village was the most difficult thing any of us has ever done."

"I can't imagine how you felt," said Parthi. "At least we have a place to go, and our entire city is with us. You set off with no one and didn't know where you were going. We have all of our people and know our destination. My friends who have been to the new Velzna say it is the most imposing site they have ever seen."

"Will we risk an attack on the way?" asked Romulus.

"That is unlikely," answered Parthi. "Our territory extends all the way to the Tiber River. The tribes to the north and south are also Etruscans. To the east, the Umbrians are our allies. We should be able to walk safely to the new city."

The road to the new Velzna was good, and at

first, it was relatively level. By nightfall, we had reached a low mountain range, and the road proceeded through them in a series of switchbacks. Talitus decided to stop for the night before we reached the steep part of the road."

Until that moment, I never thought about what was involved when thousands of people come to rest for the night. The Velznans congregated in groups ranging from a dozen to a hundred or so on the flat ground in the foothills of the mountains. Each group collected firewood, and within a short time, it looked as if a small city had appeared out of nowhere. The burning fires provided a sense of unity and security that helped put the past behind us.

The rest of the journey was uneventful. We passed through some steep hills in the morning, but we were fresh after a good sleep. Once we reached the summit of the mountains, Tanaquil pointed out the location of the new city to us.

"The mountain with the flat top is the site of our new city. I have never been there, but I am sure I am right from the descriptions that I have heard."

"She is right," said Talitus, who had joined us. "That hill is where we will make the new city of Velzna. What do you think of it?"

"I have never seen a more defensible place," said Romulus. "No enemy could scale those cliffs with fighters in the city."

"There are some cities in Greece that have

been built in similar locations," said Milo with a touch of pride. "A shortcoming of such cities is the lack of a supply of water. They are so high above the surrounding area that there are no springs on the surface."

Talitus nodded at Milo and added, "Your Greek friends said the same thing, and we heeded their words. Over the past few years, we have chiseled cisterns into the rocks to collect rainwater. In addition, we have begun digging a network of defensive caves, and from them deep wells reach the waters that flow far below the surface. When we get to the city, I will show you."

As we drew closer to Velzna, Talitus sent riders ahead of the group to tell the defenders of the outpost who we were. When we arrived, we were greeted at a distance by their banging their swords against their shields. The row of warriors standing on the crest of the plateau was a stirring sight.

The closer we got to the hill, the more imposing it became. The flat top of the mountain seemed inaccessible because the slope was so steep. It was only when we were right beside the cliff that we saw the trail to the top.

"You could not have designed a more secure position," insisted Romulus. "Only two attackers at a time could use the trail, and horses would be no help at all."

"The inaccessibility of the site is also its greatest drawback," said Sethra. "Most of our livestock have to graze on the land below the city. Our fields and pastures must also be located on the lowlands. Even so, it is an incomparable location for a city."

We did not climb to the top of the plateau that day. Talitus said that it would be pointless for the whole group to do so now. There was little protection from the elements at the top and only a few shelters. We would camp tonight on the lowlands and make temporary huts there until more permanent shelters could be built on the top of the plateau.

Many of the younger Velznans could not resist seeing what their new home would be like. After getting the approval of Sethra, they decided to hike the trail to the top, and we joined them. The climb was difficult, but when we reached the top, we understood why this site was chosen. The top of the hill, actually a small mountain, was impregnable. Attackers would have almost no chance of succeeding.

What was just as evident was the beauty of the place. From the new city of Velzna, the view of the surrounding area was stunning. The gods must have made this site for their own enjoyment, and the Velznans were blessed to have found such a place.

Chapter XXI

Returning to Olympus, Discordia found that the Keres were no longer as cordial to her as they were before. Despite her promises, they had found very few souls on which to feed.

The failure of Discordia to crush the Albans, combined with her humiliation before the other gods, drove her to desperation. She did something that would change the Keres forever by allowing them to feed on living humans.

The frustrated goddess also paid another visit to the Veiians in the guise of a mortal woman. When she informed them that the Albans were at the edge of their land, a group of warriors set out after them.

Although the Velznans, especially Talitus and Sethra, encouraged us to stay, we left the new settlement after just two days. We had several reasons for this decision, including the words of

Aranth. Most of all, we did not want our friends to suffer because a god had chosen to punish us for unknown reasons.

"If you insist on leaving us, let me suggest where you might go," said Talitus. "The land of the Umbrians is on the other side of the Tiber River, just a short walk from here. The valley between the mountains is fertile and relatively flat. None of the Etruscan tribes has claimed this land, and much of it is still wilderness. What is most important is that if you settle there, you will not be far from us."

The advice that Talitus gave us was sensible, so we headed east. We reached the river in less than an hour and found a shallow place to cross into the land of the Umbrians.

"Colder weather will be arriving soon, so I think we should head south along the river," said Remus.

"Our village is toward the south," added Nico wistfully. "I like the idea of going that way. I wonder how far it is?"

"If I remember correctly, it is more than ten days from here on foot," answered Milo.

"Maybe we can visit once we have found a place where we can live," said Nico. "After our first harvest, we can bring food when we visit."

Listening to Nico made me homesick, and I'm sure others felt the same way. This was the first time that we were close enough to our village to feel that we could visit. There was also something about being close to the Tiber River that was reassuring. We all knew that the southern part of the river was less than a day from our village, so walking beside the river was almost like being home.

Finding food was not a problem because there was still fruit on the trees. The river provided us with fish, and there were small animals we could hunt. For eight days, we walked south through the valley. We were not sure what we were looking for. Going in this direction seemed like the right thing to do, if for no other reason than the weather would be warmer.

Nivea's behavior was another reason we followed the river downstream. Whenever we found a site that seemed promising, she became agitated. We didn't understand why she was behaving in this way, but we trusted her judgment.

The most surprising thing about our journey is that we came upon only a few settlements, and none of them were inhabited. It seemed mysterious to us, but Milo had an explanation that seemed logical.

"This area is a border area where several different tribes come together. As the tribes became stronger, they challenged one another for dominance. This area is where many of the battles took place. The people who lived in the area, who were loyal to the tribe that was strongest, became tired of the conflict. They moved to places that had a larger population and were defended more readily by one of the tribes."

"I take it you don't think this would be a good place for us to settle," said Gaius.

Milo answered quickly. "In many ways, this is a perfect place because the land is fertile and not very hilly. Crops and animals would grow well here. The problem of continuing conflict, however, is not going to go away soon. It would be impractical to live here because each of the tribes would consider you an enemy. Some day, a tribe may be strong enough to control the area, and when that happens, this would be a fine place to live."

We stopped at midday to rest and eat. As we usually did, we found a protected place to stop. It was a small valley with steep sides and a few trees that provided us with shade. Water flowed from a spring to form a stream that flowed into the Tiber.

No sooner had we settled in than we heard the sounds of horses trotting. In a moment, we saw a band of warriors approaching us from the north. The lead rider was looking at the ground, which meant he was tracking us.

"They will know we are here," whispered Romulus, "so it makes no sense to hide. Be ready to fight if we are attacked, but don't provoke them. We pose no threat, we are not staying here, and there may be no reason for them to be afraid of us."

"Do you want me to talk to them?" asked Milo.

"No, that would put you in danger. Let them come to us," answered Romulus. "They might think that we are harmless travelers."

Romulus could not have been more wrong. The moment the riders saw us, they drew their weapons, urged the horses on, and headed toward us.

"Climb up the rocks!" shouted Romulus. "They will have to abandon their horses to reach us. We will hold the high ground."

The attackers had to form a single line to move between the trees and into the canyon. The first rider was completely unprepared for what happened next. Nivea, who had clambered up the rocky wall, hurled herself at the rider, knocking him from his horse. Dazed, he lay on the ground struggling futilely to get up. His horse turned in the narrow space and ran back the way it had come in, slowing the other riders.

Remus thrust his spear at one of the riders, wounding him severely. He slumped over his horse, which started walking in circles. The rest of the attackers realized that they had no chance of success on their horses in the canyon and withdrew. The last of the attackers was wounded by Chiara, who stepped from behind a tree and struck him with her sword.

The warriors grabbed their weapons and prepared to attack us on foot. One of them drew his bow and sent an arrow toward Romulus, who was standing protectively in front of Katia and

Nico. An eagle swooped down out of nowhere, deflected the arrow, and flew screaming into the face of the bowman, clawing at his eyes.

The Veiians who were uninjured retreated quickly, intimidated by our response to their attack and the mystical appearance of the eagle. They remounted their horses, but instead of renewing their attack, rode about uncertainly. Three of their warriors were struggling in the mouth of the canyon, and the bowman was kneeling on the ground clutching his eyes.

Despite the cloudless sky, a mist descended on us. Fearsome winged shapes appeared, which we recognized as the Keres. But none of the Veiians had died, so there were no souls on which they could feed. Instead, they attacked the wounded men, biting at their necks and drinking their blood.

Seeing their comrades becoming the victims of these horrible creatures, the Veiians turned their horses and escaped. Years later, we learned what our attackers did. They returned to Veii and explained what happened during our encounter. As incredible as their story sounded, they were convincing, especially when they reminded listeners about the first conflict between the Veiian attackers and the Albans. The result was that the Veiians chose to avoid any contact with us, believing that we were somehow aligned with the forces of the Underworld.

When the Keres had finished feeding on the

Veiians, they turned to us. We stood there frozen in time as they crept forward until Romulus shouted, "Stand together and keep your weapons drawn! Nivea, come with me."

Romulus grabbed a spear and walked toward the Keres. Growling fiercely, Nivea stayed by his side. Remus drew his sword and joined them.

Sucking the blood of living humans was so intoxicating that the Keres were fearless. They felt invincible and were so focused on turning the humans into their next victims that they were unaware of the faint glow that emanated from our weapons.

With a flap of its wings, one of the Keres rose into the air and launched itself at Romulus. Resting the butt of his spear on the ground, Romulus waited for the fiend, who believed it could not be harmed by human weapons. The demon impaled itself on the spear. After releasing a blood-curdling scream, the monster disintegrated into dust.

Only then did the other Keres notice the glowing weapons and detect the supernatural aura that surrounded the *gemelli* and the ever-present dog. The Keres flew off, carrying the Veiians whose blood they had drunk. To our horror, these victims were not dead. They had begun to assume the ghastly form of the Keres. Like the Keres, these undead would feed on the blood of other humans. They would be known until the end of days by a name that would strike fear in every human. They would be called vampires.

With a tired voice, Romulus said, "Let's get out of here before anything else happens. Aeneas spoke the truth when he said great challenges awaited us."

All of us felt the same weariness that Romulus did, and we were impatient to move on. As beautiful as this place was, the attack by the Veiians and the appearance of the Keres made it impossible for us to be comfortable here. We continued on our way and never looked back. In our haste to escape the memory of the Keres, we walked through the night and did not stop for rest until the sun was high the next day.

The valley of the Tiber River became wider and flatter. The river twisted through it, and in almost every bend, a small settlement had been established. The people in these settlements spoke our language, and they were loosely affiliated with Alba Longa. None of the villages seemed particularly prosperous. We didn't think any of them could support new inhabitants, no matter how hard we worked.

The event that changed our lives occurred as we drew near to one of these villages. An eagle that was soaring overhead landed in front of Nivea, who was leading our group. The bird showed no fear, nor did Nivea. This was unusual to begin with because none of us had ever seen an eagle behave like this. What made the incident even more mysterious was that it appeared, to our eyes at least, to be the same eagle that had attacked the Veiian archer. Nivea turned to us, wagged her tail, and settled down for a nap. The eagle flew just a short distance away and sat on the branch of a pine tree.

Although none of us was experienced with omens, even we recognized that this was a sign of something. "Perhaps this is where we are intended to stay," sighed Nico. "I'm really getting tired of this journey."

Smiling at Nico's comment, Romulus agreed with him. "The location is ideal, and I'm just as eager as you are to end our wandering. Those hills over there can be easily defended, and the land seems fertile."

"Let's talk to the people of the settlement," proposed Remus. "From here, it looks like they are barely getting by. But given how close they are to our home village, they might have some sympathy for us."

"May I make a suggestion?" asked Milo. "When you go, have Chiara, Nico, and Katia accompany you. I think that the villagers will be more receptive."

The four of them went to the village, and the rest of us wandered over to the banks of the river. Some boats were on the shore, and a small island was in the middle of the river. Ducks and geese floated in the river below the island, and schools of fish swam in the current. It was such a restful scene that we hoped we might enjoy it for a long time.

When Remus and the others returned, they were smiling. "The villagers said that we were welcome, and that they would like to meet us. One of the women even recognized Chiara from a time she had visited Alba Longa." He then added quickly, "Don't be too hopeful. The village is just as poor as it looks from a distance."

Chapter XXII

The safe arrival of the Albans at the settlement by the river sent Discordia into a rage. She decided that she could trust none of the demons and took matters into her own hands. She settled on a course of action that, in her mind, was foolproof.

It began with an invasion of the dreams of Remus, but it went beyond that. Once she had entered his mind, she would be able to control him. Her plan for him and Romulus was simple and deadly. When they were finished, she would deal with the rest of the Albans.

The small village beside the Tiber River had no name. The area where the village was located was called the *Septimontium* because of the seven hills that surrounded it. The village itself consisted of a handful of people living in small shelters. They grew some crops, raised a few cattle and goats, and caught fish in the river. Other villages were nearby, all of which were very similar. They were populated by a mix of Etruscans and Latins, and as we were to learn, they got along well.

Because people of the village had so little, the Veiians, who controlled much of the area across the river, left them alone. Another reason that the Veiians were so indifferent to the village was the terrain. Much of the land beside the river and between the hills was swampy. These marshes were infested with the biting insects called *musca* during the summer. There was not much land that could be grazed or cultivated. The marshes also made it difficult for horses and wagons to move easily.

When we arrived, the people of the village greeted us. Because so many travelers wandered up and down the river, they were not apprehensive about our presence. They were, however, interested in hearing why we left our home.

We explained briefly that we had to leave our village near Alba Longa because of drought and raiders. It was our hope to find a place where we might settle, and we would work for this privilege. We knew from experience that it was better to withhold the details of our adventures, particularly those involving the Veiians and creatures from the Underworld.

The leader of the village, Elianus, said, "As you

can see, we have virtually nothing to offer you other than a little food and an opportunity to settle around our village. Because it is so late in the season, you will have to work hard to get enough food to last through the winter. You may be able to exchange your labor for food with some of the other tribes."

"How will we know where we may settle?" asked Remus, who seemed taken aback by such a brief and direct answer.

"You may settle any area that is not enclosed by a fence, marked by boundary stones, or planted with crops. Our animals all share grazing land, so we would not want you to build on the flatter areas near the marsh. There are some abandoned huts at the edge of the village you may use until you have made permanent shelters. If you choose, you may renovate the huts and make them your own."

"May we consider putting our shelters on the hills above where you have built yours?" asked Romulus.

Elianus smiled and said, "If you are willing to walk up and down the hills, then you are welcome to them. You are young and enthusiastic. The hills will be less challenging for you than they are for us."

Looking around, I noticed that there were no children or teenagers in the village. I asked Elianus why, thinking they might be away doing something.

With a sad look, Elianus responded, "No, there are no young people left. Our village is so poor that all of the young people, especially parents with children, have moved to other places. I hope you don't find that too discouraging. Our village is a better place with all of you around."

Romulus spoke for all of us when he said to Elianus, "We are grateful for your offer. Some day we might find the energy to make our home on one of the hills. For now, we should probably live in the huts you mentioned."

Elianus led us to the edge of the village and showed us the huts. They seemed to be in good condition and were very much like the ones in our village. We wandered around and remembered our old homes as we got to know our new ones.

We spent a peaceful winter in our new home. It was easy to find work in the surrounding villages, and for our efforts, we were paid with food, tools, and building materials. Some of the materials were used to improve the huts we lived in, but we also put some aside for our own village that we hoped to build on one of the hills.

The people of the settlement treated us like family. I think their feelings for us were a reflection of how they felt for the young people who had left their village. I must also admit that our affection for them showed how much we missed our own families.

There were many times that winter when we

considered visiting our village. We could have been there in less than a day, and the road to Alba Longa was not far from the settlement. One evening, we sat around the fire and talked about this possibility.

"It would be wonderful to see my parents and little sister," said Katia, "but I'm not sure I could leave them again."

"My big concern is that they would be sad to see us for a day and then have to give us up again," added Gaius. "I can just see my mother trying to give me all the food she had so I would have something to eat on my return trip."

Most of us had nothing to add to the conversation, because if we did, we would probably have to choke back the tears. In the end, we all agreed that it was not yet the right time to visit our families. It was easier not knowing how they were doing. We hoped for the best rather than taking a chance on learning that they were suffering.

The situation was different with Milo. He was free to return to Cumae, and he knew that other Greeks would be trading nearby. He could join them and be back in his home in a matter of days.

"If I left Chiara even for a few days, I would feel terrible," he said. "I'll never forget what happened to her at the hands of the Arroni and Vulci." Changing his tone completely, Milo assumed a proud stance and insisted, "I could never leave all of you. What would you do without me?"

We laughed so hard that the people living in the main part of the village probably thought we had been possessed. It reminded us of other times we had laughed, and we shared some of the funny things that had happened to us. What was most important, his humor made us stop thinking about how much we missed our families.

During the spring, we began looking at the hills around the village more carefully. All of the hills had certain advantages, and we enjoyed talking about how each of them would make a good home. Three of the hills, however, were taller than the others and were closer to the river. Any one of these three would be a good site for our new village.

Romulus favored one of the hills for a reason none of us had considered. "The villagers who gave us shelter live close to this hill. If we make our settlement on this hill, we will be in a good position to protect them. I think we owe them that much."

"There is another reason to choose this hill," argued Remus. "It is more or less in the middle of the others and the villages that surround them. That makes it easier to defend."

"Before we start building, we should look for an omen," suggested Gaius. "We are in no hurry and can use the time to gather more materials."

The omen came in a few days, but unfortunately, it was not clear. A flock of six vultures flew over the hill that was farthest south and closest to the river. This seemed like a good sign to us. A short time later, however, a flock of twelve vultures flew over the hill that was more or less central.

"The first group of vultures was the omen," insisted Remus.

"But the second group was larger," countered Romulus, looking at his brother in a strange way. "When the advantages of the central hill are considered in combination with the twelve vultures, it seems to me that the omen is clear."

Elianus told us that these two hills had names. The central hill was called Palatium, because on the site, a city had been built hundreds of years before by Evander and a band of Greeks. The southern hill was called Aventium and was named after an ancient king.

"Do you believe these stories?" asked Romulus.

"Yes, I do," answered Elianus, "and there is a related story. The fire-breathing monster Cacus lived in a cave on Aventium. After defeating Geryon, Hercules was driving his cattle back to Greece. When he rested near Aventium, Cacus stole some of the cattle and hid them in his cave. Hercules broke into the sealed cave, killed the monster Cacus, and recovered the cattle."

"Such a legendary place should be our new home," argued Remus.

Regardless of what Remus said, we were still not confident about choosing the site of our village. Gaius repeated his suggestion that we were in no hurry. "Let's wait for nine days. That number is midway between six and twelve, how many vultures were in each group. At that time, we can reconsider what the vultures meant and continue looking for other omens."

Later that day, Remus drew me aside and said, "Serena, I need your help to understand my dreams. For several nights, I have slept badly. A voice is speaking to me, and I don't recognize it. The voice keeps telling me that I was born to greatness, yet Romulus is seen as our leader. For the first time that I can remember, I am becoming angry with our brother."

"It's probably nothing," I said. "We have gone through so much that I'm surprised we aren't screaming at one another. When we start to build our village, all of us will feel better."

But Remus did not feel better, and in fact, his mood worsened. The others noticed, too, because he was confrontational with everyone. He started spending more time alone on Aventium.

A storm struck one afternoon, and all of us quickly returned to our shelters, except Remus. He was on Aventium when the storm hit. We could see him from where we were, and despite the rain, wind, and lightning, he didn't seek a safe place. Instead, he appeared to be talking to a woman. She was dressed in beautiful clothes that were far different from those worn by any woman in the nearby villages.

After the storm ended, he came down from Aventium, and was more distant than ever. His dark mood was evident from his look and his behavior. When Romulus asked who the woman was, Remus scowled and snapped, "It's really none of your business."

Later, I asked him the same question. He answered, "She said she is from a nearby village and sometimes walked to Aventium. It was nice talking to her. She seemed to know all about us. I told her I wanted us to make a village on Aventium, and she said it was the best spot."

"Weren't the two of you afraid of the storm? There was so much rain and lightning, but you didn't seek shelter."

"It wasn't stormy on top of the hill," said Remus. "We could see that there were clouds and rain all around us, but the top of the hill got none of it. She said this was proof that Aventium should be our home. I agree with her."

Over the next few days, we saw Remus with this mysterious woman. None of us could get close to her, but we could see her from a distance. Whenever someone approached, she walked away quickly.

Another troubling thing happened whenever she was around. Nivea growled and never took her eyes away from Remus. At these times, she stayed close by and always stood between the woman who had befriended my brother and us.

Chapter XXIII

Her plan had worked just as Discordia had intended. Remus came to trust her, and within a few days, she had turned him against his brother.

Until now, Discordia was intent on the destruction of the Albans. Her success with Remus raised another possibility. Once Romulus was gone, Remus would become the leader of the Albans, and he could convince them to worship her. She had never been worshipped before, only feared, and her pride drove her to seek this new level of veneration.

On the morning of the ninth day, we decided to spend some time on the two hills. Nothing had happened that we could consider an omen. Maybe there would be something on one of the hills that would help us make the decision.

Over the objections of Remus, we visited Palatium first. From the crest of this hill, we could see all around us. The top was relatively flat, and there were several trails that led up from the lowland below. Using these, we could easily move the materials we had gathered to start our new settlement.

Nivea pranced around the hill as if it were her home. Romulus could not keep from describing what he thought the settlement would look like once we had finished. He and Chiara made us laugh as they positioned us to outline the wall that he insisted the settlement would need when it became a city. Once we were in position, he dragged a stick from one person to another so we could see where the wall would be.

We were so distracted by this undertaking that we didn't notice the woman standing beside Remus. She spoke to Remus loudly enough so that we all could hear.

"Look what your brother has done, Remus. The signs all say that your choice, Aventium, was meant to be your new home. But he has created the *pomerium*, the sacred boundary for your settlement, on Palatium."

"I did no such thing," insisted Romulus. "There was no ceremony and no sacrifice. I expected to do the same on Aventium. And who are you, to interfere in matters that are not your business? We have asked permission of Elianus and his people, and they have given us their approval to build here."

"Who am I, you ask?" queried the woman. "I

am Discordia, the goddess of strife, and your brother is under my control."

The top of the hill became stormy, and the air around us swirled violently. The woman was transformed into a goddess who was both beautiful and horrible to behold. Her hair turned into a mass of snakes with blood dripping from their mouths. She held her hand out, and Remus drew his sword. Looking at him, she commanded, "Kill Romulus."

Romulus rushed to within several steps of Remus and pleaded, "She has possessed you, brother. Do not do this thing. Drop your sword. I will not defend myself."

We could see that Remus was trying to fight the spell. His movements were strained, and he clutched the sword awkwardly. The grimace on his face showed the inner agony he must be experiencing.

Only two steps separated the brothers. Remus held his sword over his shoulder and prepared to plunge it into Romulus. As he promised, Romulus did not try to defend himself. Instead, he stood there waiting for death. Discordia waved her hand and said, "I am lifting the spell, because it is too late to stop Remus. I want him to kill his brother in full control of his consciousness."

The look of horror on his face showed that Remus was free of Discordia's enchantment. He understood what he was about to do, but he seemingly could not stop himself. Then, with a mighty force of will, he changed his position slightly. He grabbed the blade, allowed the hilt to hit the ground, and fell on the sword. It passed right through him, and he died instantly.

Nivea threw herself at Discordia, and a dark mist enveloped both of them. We could not see what happened, but from the sounds, we knew a titanic struggle was going on. An intense storm came out of nowhere as if sent by Aeolus, the keeper of the winds, and blew the mist away.

Discordia was kneeling on the ground screaming with her hands covering her face. The snakes entwined in her hair were striking her again and again. Nivea stood in front of her growling fiercely. The ground under Discordia opened, and she fell into a fiery abyss. When she was gone, the ground closed up around her.

Romulus rushed to his brother, pulled the sword from him, and clutched him in his arms. Silent and in tears, I hugged both of them. It was the worst moment of my life, made even more tragic by Nivea's mournful howling.

Through my tears, I could see the air around us begin to radiate a light that was somehow peaceful. My sadness eased, and a figure appeared before us. It was Aeneas. The spirit of Remus rose from his body and stood beside Aeneas.

"As I said when I saw you last, the Fields of Elysium are waiting for those mortals who have lived a brave and righteous life. I will escort your brother's spirit there, for he has shown courage and virtue, as have all of you. The heinous Discordia, who drove your brother to this unimaginable act, could not overcome his goodness and love for you. She will pay dearly for what she has done."

Although the spirit of Remus did not speak to us, we could recognize in our souls that he would always be with us. The two of them faded away, and the despair that had filled our heart was replaced with elation. We have missed him every day, but we know that he is in the sublime presence of the blessed.

Struggling to his feet, Romulus spoke solemnly. "There can be no more convincing sign that this should be our future home than what has happened today. On this spot, my brother gave his life to spare mine and was taken to the Fields of Elysium by Aeneas. Our nemesis, Discordia, has been punished by greater gods. This ground is sacred and should be revered by us and our descendants."

All of us looked at Romulus with a deep sense of commitment. This would be our home, and to signify our agreement, we raised our hands in salute. The decision was made.

Our first duty now was to bury Remus with honor. It was Chiara who proposed Aventium as the burial site. "The birds gave us two signs. One was for our new home, and now we understand that the other was for the resting place of Remus. In addition, Hercules had a triumph there. The remains of Remus were meant for Aventium."

We made a bier of two spears with branches laid across them to carry his body. Gaius and Milo ran to our huts and brought digging tools to Aventium. In the cleft between the two peaks of the hill were several caves. The body of Remus and the knife he always carried were placed respectfully in a hole we dug at the back of one of the smaller caves. After covering his body, we filled the cave with stones. Rather than marking the cave, we disguised it as well as we could by moving a huge rock over the opening. Those of us who knew the site never disclosed its location to anyone. To the day of this writing, no one else has discovered the burial place of Remus.

As we returned to the village, we saw that Elianus and the others were waiting for us. The expressions on their faces were difficult to read.

"How much should we tell them?" I asked Romulus.

"I'm not sure," he answered. "I guess it depends on how much they saw and understood."

Katia begged, "Whatever you say, please don't make them send us away."

"What happened up there?" asked Elianus. "The top of the mountain became stormy, so we couldn't see well. From here, it looked like Remus confronted Romulus, who then killed him. We thought it had something to do with the woman who has been seen with Remus."

"That is not what happened at all," answered

Chiara quickly. What she said next was a very convincing lie. "As you know, Remus wanted to settle on Aventium. While we were at the top of the hill, he sacrificed a boar with his sword to prove he was right. The signs said we should settle on Palatium, and he became upset. He left with the woman, saying they would join her clan. This was not unexpected, because he was becoming closer to the woman."

"But what about the body that you carried to Aventium?" asked one of the village women.

Without hesitation, Chiara continued with her deception. "What you saw was the body of the sacrificed boar. We did not want to offend the gods in case we misread the signs, so we buried the boar on Aventium. If Remus ever returns, we can show him that we honored his choice, and we will treat the hill that was his choice with respect."

Chiara's story was believable, or so we thought. As we would find out later, there were some skeptics in the group of villagers. They spread a different story: that Romulus had killed Remus. Shepherds and farmers from other villages had also seen the incident, and they, too, believed that one twin had killed the other. This was the story that was spread far and wide. To this day, it is the one that is known by most people.

After speaking with Elianus and the villagers, we went back to our huts. The events of the morning had drained us, and for a time, we just sat around gloomily. Romulus brought us out of our melancholy with a suggestion.

"Does anyone want to go up to Palatium with me? We have been through every ordeal imaginable, and our antagonist, Discordia, has been banished to who knows where. I want to start building our new home now!"

Without a moment's hesitation, all of us stood up. A spirit of renewal swept over us. We picked up our tools and started toward the hill. We paused only to pick up the building materials we could carry. Romulus ran to our shelter, grabbed something, and raced Milo to the top. Nivca barked to urge us on, swept up with our new excitement.

"Let's put some boundary stones at the corners," directed Romulus. "Use the outline that we made before."

There were stones of all sizes on the top of the mountain. We could have used small stones, but we didn't. Working in small teams, we rolled the biggest stones we could to the corners. Not satisfied with that, we stacked at least one more stone on top of the first one. This was truly a labor of love.

After the boundary stones were in place, we walked around the perimeter of our new settlement. Each family group chose a spot for its shelter. We planned the common areas that we all would share and even marked the trail that we would turn into a road.

"None of us knows the ceremony needed to mark the *pomerium*, but I think we should try," said Romulus. He pulled a small pottery flask from his tunic and said, "This is olive oil that Sethra gave me before we left. I think it would be fitting to pour it along our boundary."

"Who should do it?" I asked.

Chiara pushed Nico forward. "It should be Nico," she insisted. "He is the youngest, and if he offends the gods, they won't punish him harshly."

We cheered her decision, and Nico proudly accepted the flask from Romulus. With as much solemnity as he could summon, he walked along the boundary line pouring the oil.

After the last drop touched the ground, the most wondrous thing happened. Nivea, who had been sitting quietly as Nico performed the ceremony, started glowing. The brightness embraced all of us, and Nivea was transformed into the goddess Juno. We fell to the ground and were afraid to look up.

"Stand and look at me, my children. Though you faced the most perilous challenges, you have succeeded and brought honor to me and all of the immortals. I have been with you as Nivea since the birth of the *gemelli*, knowing that you would be treated harshly at the hands of Discordia. Through it all, you have persevered and have created an enduring legacy."

"Thank you, most esteemed Juno," said Romulus with humility and deference. "Words cannot express our appreciation for your protection and for your friendship in the form of Nivea. Until this moment, none of us could understand Nivea's uncommon abilities. Never has there been a finer or more protective companion. Your presence in her has been a gift without equal."

Gathering his courage, Nico asked in a timid voice, "Will we ever see our families again?"

"Your families will join you one day soon, and they will add to the prominence of the city you will build." Looking at Romulus, Juno smiled and said, "You have one more question for me, don't you?"

"Will those who come after us know our story?" he asked.

"In the course of time, the village that you build on this spot will become a resplendent city that rivals Olympus in beauty. Your story will never be forgotten, and for a hundred generations or more, this unmatched city will represent the best of humanity."

With a wave of her hand, Juno created a vision that took our breath away. The most incredible structures of every kind appeared on the hills and lowlands around us. Elegant buildings, arenas, temples, and monuments of brick and marble stretched as far as we could see. Throngs of people walked the streets, and their dignity was the perfect match for the beauty and majesty of the city.

As the vision faded, so did Juno. Her spirit remained in all of us, and for the rest of our lives, there was never a moment that we were without her. We missed Nivea, of course, but it was not long before neighboring shepherds brought us puppies. They have now grown into great, white dogs that remind us both of Nivea and our protector, Juno.

Everyone in the villages that encircled Palatium also saw the vision that we experienced. They came together with us, wanting to be part of the destiny that Juno promised. Our settlement was successful, and as Juno promised, we were eventually reunited with our families.

The settlement still has no name. Some of the people from across the river who speak Etruscan call it *Ruma*, which has become a joke among us. We accuse Romulus of consorting with them to name the village after him. The truth is, however, that he would be embarrassed by any special attention that is paid to him.

The first structure we built on Palatium was a stone altar to Juno. Chiara and Milo were married in a ceremony before the altar. A year later, the first baby in our village was born to them. They named him Julius, and he is already showing signs of the brashness and bravery of his parents.

Despite his young age, Romulus became the leader of the settlement. He has ruled wisely, seeking advice from others and avoiding the lust for power that has corrupted so many. And every day that he is here, he walks from Palatium to Aventium. He places his hand on a large stone that has come to be called Remoria and remembers the brother who shared our destiny.

Interesting Stuff about the Author

Michael Milone lives in a beautiful part of New Mexico with his wife, Sheri, two dogs, and lots of cats. They have a xeriscape garden that is mostly native plants and requires little water. Birds and desert animals enjoy their garden, and among their visitors is a bobcat family.

Every day begins with running, biking, swimming, or working out at the gym. He has completed 35 marathons, including Boston, two Ironman races, and hundreds of other races. In the winter, he goes skiing or snowboarding when he can. One of his favorite events is the Mt. Taylor Winter Quadrathlon, which includes biking, running, cross country skiing, and snowshoeing. The course is more than 40 miles long and goes up and down a mountain that is 11,301 feet high.

The Boring Stuff

Dr. Michael Milone is a nationally recognized research psychologist and award-winning educational writer. He earned a Ph.D. in 1978 from The Ohio State University and has served in an adjunct capacity at Ohio State, the University of Arizona, Gallaudet University, and New Mexico State University. He has taught in regular and special education programs at all levels, holds a Master of Arts degree from Gallaudet University, and is fluent in American Sign Language. He was a regular contributor to *Technology & Learning* magazine and currently serves on the Research Advisory Board of Renaissance Learning and the Education Advisory Team of Bluenose Edutainment.

Questions and Answers

For more information, visit junostwins.com.

When and where does the story take place?

The story takes place around 800 BC. If you believe the legends, the exact date of the founding of Rome is April 21, 753 BC. You have to admire a legend that has such a precise date.

The location of the story is central Italy. The map in the front of the book shows the main places mentioned in the story.

Almost all the places named in *Juno's Twins* existed at the time the story took place. You can visit these places to learn about the ruins from thousands of years ago and see how the towns look now. A few of the place names are made up, including Fontis, Apia, and Pontia.

The dedication line at the beginning of the book says FACERE OPERAE PRETIUM. What does this mean?

These three words are my favorite Latin quote. They can be interpreted in a few ways, but the one I like best is "to do worthy things." They appear in the preface to *The History of Rome* written by Titus Livius. He was born in northern Italy around 59 BC and died in 17 AD.

Livy, as he is known in English, wrote the words about himself. He wasn't being boastful and didn't expect fame or fortune to come from his work. In fact, he was describing his effort to do something useful by making known the achievements of the great people who came before him.

Many people already know the tale of Romulus and Remus. Why did you mess around with the story?

When I was young, my Italian grandmother told me the story of Romulus, Remus, and the founding of Rome. In that version of the story, which is the most well-known (there are others), Romulus and Remus argued about where Rome should be built, and Romulus killed Remus. I thought that was a terrible thing to do, especially because I have a brother. I decided there had to be a better way to tell the story.

Were Romulus and Remus real people?

There is no evidence that Romulus and Remus existed. That doesn't mean that they didn't exist, or that they didn't live in the settlement that became Rome. It just means that scientists haven't found the evidence needed to prove they were real people.

You might wonder how we know if anyone who lived around three thousand years ago was real. Archeologists and historians learn about ancient people through writings, paintings, and historic artifacts from the time the people lived. Sometimes there is a lot of evidence. This is why we know so much about Egypt, Greece, and Rome.

Why haven't we heard more about Discordia? She's such an evil goddess that she should be famous.

Discordia is more famous under another name, Eris. Discordia is the Roman name for Eris, who was originally a Greek goddess. The Romans borrowed many of their myths from the Greeks. This sharing of stories was very common among early humans, especially those who lived around the Mediterranean Sea.

There is no question about Discordia being a very evil goddess. She might be considered the original "mean girl." The Greeks and Romans thought that this goddess was responsible for everything from family members squabbling with one another to great wars.

What kind of dog was Nivea?

The extraordinary dog Nivea in the story was a Maremma. This wonderful breed of dog is thousands of years old and is still used today for watching over herds of animals like sheep and goats. They are smart, friendly, and loyal dogs that are good watchdogs without being aggressive.

Were the Albans real people?

It is likely that people have lived in the place called Alba Longa for many thousands of years. In that respect, the Albans were real people. The area has good soil, water sources, and can be defended. The climate in that part of Italy is temperate, and the scenery is beautiful.

Some legends say that people from Alba Longa founded the city of Rome. This may or may not be true. Given how close Alba Longa is to Rome, it is likely that some people who lived in Alba Longa made their way to Rome.

Who were the Etruscans?

The people that we call Etruscans are among the most mysterious civilizations in all of history. They left behind many ruins, weapons, works of art, and household objects, but not many written texts that we can understand. Most of what we know about them comes from their grave sites called *necropolis*. They were strong believers in the afterlife and made elaborate tombs.

If you ever find yourself in Rome, be sure to visit Villa Giulia, the National Etruscan Museum. This is my favorite museum in the whole world. It is at the edge of a beautiful park, and it has a fabulous collection of art and artifacts from Etruscan times. Best of all, this museum is almost never crowded.